P9-DFX-932

# SHIPWRECK ISLAND

# SHIPWRECK ISLAND

S. A. BODEEN

FEIWEL AND FRIENDS
NEW YORK

A FEIWEL AND FRIENDS BOOK
An Imprint of Macmillan


Printed in the United States of America by R. R. Donnelley & Sons Company, Harrisonburg, Virginia. For information, address Feiwel and Friends, 175 Fifth Avenue, New York, N.Y. 10010.

Feiwel and Friends books may be purchased for business or promotional use. For information on bulk purchases, please contact the Macmillan Corporate and Premium Sales Department at (800) 221-7945 x5442 or by e-mail at specialmarkets@macmillan.com.

Library of Congress Cataloging-in-Publication Data Available

ISBN: Hardcover – 978-1-250-02777-1 / Ebook – 978-1-250-06323-6

Book design by Anna Booth

Feiwel and Friends logo designed by Filomena Tuosto

First Edition: 2014

10 9 8 7 6 5 4 3 2 1

mackids.com

*For my parents, who raised me in*
*an old house full of books*

# 1

Sarah Robinson had been ordered to pack a suitcase and, to the best of her ability, she was going to use that task to express her displeasure at the mess her life had become. She yanked a zebra-striped swimsuit and several pairs of underwear out of her top drawer. *Slam!*

A few weeks earlier, her father had married a flight attendant that he'd met through an online dating service. Sarah had held out hope that when he actually met the woman, he wouldn't like her. But when he came back from his first trip to visit her in Texas, he told Sarah, "After your mother died, I never thought I'd be happy again. But I've fallen in love. I know you'll love her too."

"Well, that's not *ever* gonna happen." Sarah hurled

the clothes at the open suitcase on her bed and opened up another drawer. She jerked out a pair of jeans. *Slam!*

On the second trip to Texas, he proposed. And then, on the third, he married her. Of course, he tried to get Sarah to go along, but she refused, insisting on staying home with her grandparents because she truly believed her father would never go through with the wedding unless she was there.

But he did. And then he and his new wife went on a short honeymoon trip before he flew home.

Sarah's new stepmother came with baggage: two new stepbrothers for Sarah. Her father had told her over the phone, "The youngest is ten, and he is just a hoot. And the other is twelve, just like you. You two have so much in common."

"The only thing we have in common is our age." Sarah twisted the jeans up and hurled them at her suitcase. She pulled out another drawer and dug into a pile of shorts, snatching up three pairs. *Slam!*

The three of them, the Murillo family, had taken a few weeks to sell their home and pack up, so they arrived the day before and had already settled, somewhat, into the Robinsons' extravagant Southern California home. Sarah took one look at their worn luggage and figured it all out.

Her new stepmother was after her dad's money. *Classic.*

"She's just a golddigger." Sarah walked into her closet and began plucking shirts off hangers with so much force that some of the hangers broke and fell on the floor. She backed out of her closet and used her foot to kick the door shut. *Slam!*

Sarah walked over to her bed, held the shirts over her head, and heaved them into the suitcase. She grabbed a hanger off the floor and whirled around, knocking some things off her dresser and onto the floor.

"Oh no!" She quickly bent to pick up a gold and glass perfume flacon, and then sighed with relief when she saw it was unbroken. She held it up to her nose and breathed in. White Shoulders. Her mother's scent.

Also on the floor was a silver frame, which she snatched up. "Oh, Mama . . ." The photograph inside was of the two of them on Heritage Day in kindergarten. Sarah's long, black hair was in loop braids, and her blue silk kimono had come from her mother's trip to Japan to visit relatives. Less than a year later, her mother was gone. Sarah slid into a heap on the floor beside her bed and set the frame in her lap. "If you were here, none of this would even be happening." She buried her face in her hands.

But tears wouldn't even come, because she was too angry to cry. This was so unlike her, to be banging and crashing about. But at the moment, she was too mad to worry about the mess she'd made.

The worst, the absolute *worst*, was the reason why she was packing.

The night before, at the newly merged family's first dinner together, Sarah had been at her usual place at the dining room table, to the right of her father, who sat at the head. John Robinson was a tall man, and very fit from playing tennis every morning before heading to work at his construction company. He wore black-rimmed glasses that made his blue eyes appear bluer, and his blond hair was nearly white in places, bleached from the California sun. Though Sarah told him it wasn't cool, he preferred to wear polo shirts and khakis nearly all the time. Sarah had inherited his chin and his dimples, but everything else—black hair and dark eyes and small frame—came right from her mother.

Sarah's new stepmother pulled out the chair across from Sarah and sat down. Yvonna Murillo was as beautiful as the models in fashion magazines. Actually more beautiful, Sarah had to admit, given all the rampant airbrushing that went on. Her eyes were darker than dark, her long hair the same, and her nose and lips were perfect, like someone had painted them. Yvonna wore a flowered sundress that showed off her muscular arms and slim figure, which, apparently, had gotten that way from playing tennis nearly as much as Sarah's father.

But Sarah needed no reminding that the beautiful woman across the table from her was her new stepmother—thus, her enemy. Sarah scowled. "That's my mom's chair."

"Sarah." Her dad narrowed his eyes at her. "Please stop."

Yvonna's forehead wrinkled as she jumped up. She sounded like she wanted to be helpful as she said, "I can sit somewhere else."

"No. Please stay where you are." John set a hand on Yvonna's arm and she sat back down. He told Sarah, "That was rude."

"It's true!" Sarah blurted. "That's where Mom always sat."

"Sarah." Her dad lowered his voice. "I know that. But things have changed."

"Yeah, I noticed." Sarah crossed her arms and leaned back in her chair, blinking back angry tears. She glared farther down the table, where her two new stepbrothers sat next to each other. Nacho, the younger one, retained some baby fat. His dark hair was in a short, little-kid haircut that made him look younger than ten, and his white Dallas Cowboys T-shirt had some kind of dark stain on the sleeve.

Chocolate from the look of it, thought Sarah. Like he'd eaten a Snickers bar and then wiped his mouth on his sleeve.

He noticed her staring at him and he glanced down. His eyes widened and he jumped up. "I need to change my shirt."

"Nacho," said Yvonna. "It's fine. Just sit."

"But I forgot to wash my hands." He pushed his chair back.

His older brother grabbed the chair. "Just sit, dude." Marco had the same color hair as his brother, only his was longer and seemed purposely unkempt, the same as a lot of boys at Sarah's school. His orange shirt bore a graphic of bull's horns, and the words *DON'T MESS WITH TEXAS.*

With a huff, Nacho plopped back down in the chair, scowling.

Both boys had their mother's eyes and nose, although Nacho's cheeks were chubbier.

John stuck a black plastic spatula into the flowered casserole dish in the middle of the table, then plopped something on her plate. Sarah sat forward to appraise the rolled-up tortilla smothered with a red sauce and melted cheese. "What is that?" she asked.

Her father answered, "Yvonna's enchiladas."

Nacho piped up, "They're the best."

Sarah glared at him for a moment, and then asked the question that had been on her mind for quite some time. "Is he seriously named after a food?"

Yvonna's dark eyes sparkled as she laughed. "No, not at all. He's named after my grandfather, Ignacio." She looked at Marco. "But Marco couldn't pronounce it. He called the baby Nacho. And it stuck." She smiled at Nacho. "Now I only call him Ignacio when he's in trouble."

Marco held up his plate. "Can we eat now?" The boys passed their plates down, and their mother loaded them up.

Sarah stared down at her dinner. "I don't like spicy food."

Under the table, her dad nudged her foot. She looked up at him, and he widened his eyes at her.

She sighed. "Fine." Sarah glared at her plate.

Everyone else began digging in with gusto, and John issued a "Yum, these are great," before taking another large bite.

Sarah's stomach growled. She doubted her dad would

put up with her going into the kitchen and making a peanut butter sandwich, so she picked up her fork and took the smallest bite possible. The sauce wasn't too spicy after all. And who could complain about melted cheese? She ate another bite.

"See?" said her dad. "Good, huh?"

Sarah didn't want to admit she liked it. So instead of answering, she shrugged. "What's in the middle?"

Yvonna smiled. "My special roasted chicken."

Sarah dropped her fork onto the plate with a loud *clink*. Then she wrapped both hands around her throat, pretending to choke. "But I'm a vegetarian!"

John set his fork down. "Since when?!"

Sarah chugged half her glass of water, wiped her mouth with the back of her hand, and then set the glass back down. "Last week." She pulled apart the sides of her white zippered hoodie to reveal a black T-shirt with the word *PETA* scrawled across it. "I'm not eating this."

Her dad rolled his eyes at Sarah and told Yvonna, "I'm so sorry."

"It's okay." Yvonna set her hand on his. "Maybe we should go ahead and tell them."

"Tell us what?" asked Sarah and Marco at the same time. They glanced at each other before quickly looking away.

John smiled at Yvonna. "Well, every wedding deserves a honeymoon."

Marco's groan was quite loud and very intentional. "Really?" he asked. "Do we have to hear about it?"

A spontaneous giggle threatened to pop out, but Sarah stifled it just in time.

Yvonna shushed Marco. "You'll want to hear this."

"Well, we planned the trip for just the two of us," John continued, "but we know this has been a whirlwind, us all moving in together. And quite an adjustment for everyone. So we thought, instead of it just being a honeymoon for two"—he reached over and set a hand on Yvonna's cheek—"that we should all go and get to know one another. So this morning, we changed our reservations and we're taking you three with us!"

"What?" Sarah screeched. She jumped to her feet and pointed at the boys. "I don't want to go anywhere with them!"

Marco blurted out, "Like we'd go anywhere with you!"

Nacho raised his hand. "I want to go."

Marco rolled his eyes and said, "Mom, I'm not going."

John said, "This is not an option. We've already booked the flights and the cruise." He tapped the table. "Sarah, sit down."

*Flights? Cruise?* Sarah didn't feel like sitting down. The only thing she felt like doing was crawling under the table and hiding. But her legs threatened to give out, so she collapsed onto her chair.

What was happening? She didn't even want to ride to the grocery store with these people, let alone some kind of long, arduous journey across half the planet.

"Where are we going?" asked Nacho.

Both Sarah and Marco glared at him as Yvonna answered. "Fiji."

John added, "Once we're there, we'll take a five-day cruise among the islands."

Sarah had been on a family cruise to Alaska the summer before. There had been tons of other kids to hang out with, she'd barely seen her dad the whole trip, and she was clinging to the hope that this cruise would be similar. Maybe she wouldn't even have to see her new family the entire trip.

The two adults gazed at each other and smiled.

Sarah wanted to throw up.

Yvonna said, "We've reserved a sailboat just for us five, with our own crew to take us on a private cruise."

Before Sarah had a chance to protest, Marco blurted out, "Are you kidding me? A stupid sailboat?"

"Marco!" Yvonna's eyes narrowed and she pointed

at him. "You are being rude. We're all going, so stop being this way."

Nacho raised his hand. "I want to go on the sail-boat."

Sarah yelled, "I'm not going! And you can't make me." She stomped to her room and had stayed there until morning, when her father had barged in. "Sarah, you will pack your suitcase and pack it now or I will pack it for you. Understand?"

Which was how Sarah found herself sitting on her floor beside her bed, wishing she could do something about the fact that she was about to embark on a trip with the new family she wanted nothing whatsoever to do with. And she was furious because she knew there was absolutely nothing she could do to keep it from hap-pening.

# 2

Marco Murillo sat on one of his new twin beds in his new room in his new home with his new stepfamily, listening to the slamming going on in the room next to his.

He wondered what that stupid girl had to be mad about.

When their parents married, she hadn't lost a thing.

Marco, on the other hand, had been forced to leave *everything* behind in Texas: his friends, his house, his school, tae kwon do, his soccer team, which was going for their fourth straight league championship . . . the list could go on and on and on.

With a huff, Marco kicked his suitcase shut. He didn't have to pack, because they had arrived only the day before, and he hadn't yet *un*packed. He knew what was going on. He knew *exactly* what was going on. His new stepfather was one of those rich guys who *bought* younger, beautiful wives. They used their money to make themselves look strong and powerful. And his mom had been sucked in.

His younger brother opened the door and strolled in, wheeling a red suitcase behind him.

"You could knock," said Marco.

"Didn't feel like it," said Nacho. He left the suitcase by the door and plopped onto the other bed and bounced a bit. "My room is just like this. Only it's light blue." He frowned. "Actually, it's almost a turquoise. Yours is dark blue. More like a navy."

Marco rolled his eyes. "I noticed."

"Did you see the pool? This house is really clean. Mom says they have a housekeeper." Nacho nodded. "Yeah, this place is way way *way* better than ours."

Marco had to agree. Since their dad had died in a car accident when Marco was barely two, the three of them had to live on their mom's salary. She wanted them to go to a decent school and live in a good neighborhood, so their house in Texas had been small. But he felt that saying so aloud would be disloyal to his old life, which he already missed. So he didn't say a word.

They heard a crash from next door.

Nacho sighed. "Our new sister sounds ticked off."

"She's not our new sister!" snapped Marco, his face growing hot. "Don't ever call her that again."

"But Mom and John are married now, so that makes her—"

"Our stepsister," finished Marco. "And the only thing that makes her that is a dumb piece of paper." He shook his head. "She's not our family. Her dad is not our family. *Mom* is our family. *You and me* are family. Got it?"

Nacho tilted his head. "But we're all a family now. Mom said."

"No." Marco sighed. "This won't last. We'll be back in Texas by the time you start fifth grade."

Nacho's eyes widened. "But that's this fall."

"Exactly." Marco smiled at the thought, hoping he was right: that the new marriage, this whole new arrangement, wouldn't last the summer.

There was a knock on the door. "Boys?" Their mom peeked in. Her hair was up in a ponytail and she wore a pink sundress. She smiled. "May I come in?" She stepped inside and sat on the end of the bed by Nacho. "Are you all packed?"

Marco frowned and pointed at his suitcase.

"Oh, sweetie." His mom reached across the space

between the two beds and set a hand on his knee. "I know this is an adjustment, but it'll get easier."

Marco stood up and walked over to the dresser. "Whatever."

Nacho said, "He says John and Sarah aren't our family."

Marco glared at Nacho.

Yvonna frowned at Marco. "Why would you say that?"

"Because they're not," said Marco. "How long did you know him before you married him? A month?"

"Stop," said his mom. "You just stop. We knew each other nearly a year."

Marco rolled his eyes. "Oh yeah, I forgot. What, you saw each other like twice?"

His mom shook her head. "I know I can't make you understand, but sometimes . . . you just *know*. You know the person is the right one for you."

Marco pointed at Nacho. "What about Nacho? Is John the right person for him?" He set a hand on his chest. "Or me? Is John the right person for me?"

His mom scratched her head and didn't say anything for a moment. The silence was not a happy one. Finally, sounding very confident, she said, "I thought about this a long time. Really hard. I love John. And I know it won't be easy at first, but this is a good move for us. He makes a very good living, so I'm retiring. No more flying. I can be a full-time mom for both of you. You'll both go to the same private school as Sarah—"

*Slam!*

"Speak of the—" Marco stopped when he saw the withering look his mother was sending his way. So Marco jerked a thumb in the direction of the sound. "What about her? You gonna be a mom for her too?"

For the first time, Marco saw the confidence on his mom's face falter. "Mom, I'm sorry, I didn't mean—"

His mom stood up and smoothed down her dress. "It's okay. That is going to be the tough part of this." She smiled. "Remember, you two have each other. Sarah is alone in this. We all have to remember that. So just . . . try to be understanding, okay?" She kissed Nacho's head, and then headed over for Marco. She put both hands on his cheeks. "Please? Try to get along?"

He nodded and she kissed his forehead.

After she left, Marco looked at Nacho. "You all packed?"

Nacho nodded.

Marco had a feeling and went over to Nacho's suitcase. He pushed it over and unzipped. "Seriously?" Three large bottles of hand sanitizer took up one half of the suitcase; the other half was full of Eco-Scout paraphernalia: manuals and rope and compasses. "What about clothes?"

Nacho shrugged. "I need that stuff more."

Marco shook his head. "No, no, no." He sighed. "Let's go pack things you'll actually need."

"I do need them! I need to keep earning badges." Nacho narrowed his eyes at his older brother.

Marco picked up the sash, which bore exactly three badges: reading, computers, and math. "Looks like you've got most of the indoor ones already."

Nacho grabbed the sash. "I've been studying all the outdoor ones. I'll take the tests when I'm ready."

"Okay, well, you do realize that you actually have to *go* outdoors to get the outdoor badges?" Marco glanced at the bottles of hand sanitizer. As long as there was dirt in the outdoors, there was no way his little brother was going to be earning any of those badges.

"I know!" Nacho reached in the back pocket of his shorts and pulled out a folded piece of notebook paper. He opened it. "On this trip, I should be able to knock out several badges." He held up a finger. "Sailing." He held up another finger. "Water safety." He held up a third finger. "Astronomy." And a fourth. "Oceanography."

Marco held up a hand to stop him. "Is there a badge for packing? Because if there is, you're not getting it." He stood the suitcase up and wheeled it out the door.

"Hold on!" Nacho refolded the paper, stuck it back in his pocket, and ran after his brother.

# 3

A Tuesday morning, the start of summer, and the airport was packed. Sarah wondered how many other kids were being dragged on trips they didn't want to go on. Looking around, she could pick out a few with scowls on their faces, obviously in the same horrid mood as she was.

"Sarah!" called her dad from the ticket counter. "Put your suitcase up on the scale so they can weigh it."

Sarah glared at Marco, who stood directly in her way. "Move."

He hardly budged, so she offered no apology of any kind as she rolled her heavy suitcase over his foot, causing him to utter a loud "Hey, that hurt!"

Their parents were too busy conferring with the gate

agent to notice, and Sarah grinned to herself as she wheeled her bag to the front of the line. Her father lugged it onto the scale, where it registered exactly 50.7 pounds. The gate agent, a man with a large head and tiny eyes, wearing the blue suit and tie of the airline, glanced at the amount and declared, "Over. That's an extra fee."

"What?" Her dad leaned over and read the numbers. "You're going to charge me for that?"

The gate agent's tiny eyes nearly disappeared as he stared down Sarah's father and nodded crisply.

"Dad, hold on." Sarah opened the outside pocket on the suitcase, extracted an extremely well-worn hardback edition of *Harry Potter and the Sorcerer's Stone,* then zipped it back up.

Her dad frowned. "Where's your e-reader?"

"In here." Sarah patted her backpack. "But you never know." As she let go of the suitcase, the numbers recalibrated, reading slightly less than forty-nine pounds. "There."

Her dad raised his eyebrows at her and then told the agent. "I booked seats together. Why does this have us in separate seats?"

Sarah quickly piped up, "I'm fine sitting by myself."

Her father ignored her and waited as the gate agent

typed on his computer. "Sir, you're trading in two first-class for five in coach at the last minute. There's only so much I can do." The agent typed on his computer for a few moments, punctuated with a few frowns, and finally said, "We can seat two together and three together." He looked up. "To even get you all on the same flight, I had to put you on an entirely different route. We have you going through Shanghai, then to Sydney, and your flight to Fiji. And this is a very full flight. Sorry about the inconvenience."

The gate agent didn't seem to be sorry about it at all, thought Sarah. Not in the least.

Her father said, "That'll have to do."

Sarah smiled. She and her dad would be together, allowing her to pretend they were simply on a trip together, alone, just like always. Her dad waved his arm. "Boys, bring your bags over."

Sarah stepped aside as her stepbrothers rolled their bags forward, not wanting to risk retaliation for rolling over Marco's foot. She shoved her book inside her bag, already wondering what movie she would watch on the plane while her dad slept beside her and she pretended the whole marriage/stepfamily debacle had been nothing but a bad dream.

When everyone had checked their bags, they went

through security with little trouble, then found their gate and sat down. Sarah told her dad, "I'm gonna go buy a magazine and some snacks."

Yvonna jumped up. "I'll come with you."

Sarah didn't say anything as she twirled around and headed for the closest shop. She sensed Yvonna behind her, but wasn't exactly in the mood to chitchat. She browsed through the section of entertainment magazines and chose two before walking over to the snack section. She grabbed a bottle of water out of the refrigerated case and let it slam before opening it again to snag a string cheese. She picked out a bag of trail mix, some yogurt pretzels, and two granola bars dipped in chocolate. There was a line at the cash register, where a pretty, dark-haired woman in a sari was checking people out. When Sarah finally reached the counter, she dumped out her goods and threw a green package of gum on top.

"I've got this," said Yvonna. She handed a bank card to the woman.

Sarah glanced at the card, which had green swirls and the logo of the California bank her dad used.

The woman asked, "Debit or credit?"

Yvonna smiled. "Debit."

Sarah said, "You bank at the same bank as my dad."

Her stepmother stiffened and didn't say anything as

she punched in her code. The woman handed her the card and receipt.

Sarah grabbed the bag of her things and could barely keep up with Yvonna on the way back to their gate. "Why do you bank at the same bank? You just moved here. How did you—" Sarah felt her face get hot as her steps slowed down. Her stepmother didn't have an account at the same bank as her dad . . . Sarah stopped in her tracks. Her stepmother had the same *account* as her dad.

About fifteen yards ahead of her, Yvonna had reached the gate and taken a seat. John smiled at her, then stood up and walked toward Sarah, who was still frozen in place. As he reached her, he started to ask something, but she blurted out, "You gave her your debit card?"

The smile on her dad's face fell, and he said, "I didn't give her my debit card."

Sarah held up her plastic shopping bag. "But she just paid for my stuff with it! She must have taken it from you and—"

"Sarah!" her dad interrupted. "Yvonna didn't take my card. She has her own."

"At your bank?" I asked.

He nodded. "Yes, at my bank. From my account."

Sarah stomped her foot. "How could you do that? Give her our money like that!"

"Listen to me, young lady." Her dad stuck his finger at her. "Yvonna is my wife. We've been married nearly a month already. Of course I'm going to share our money—my money—with her. What's mine is hers. And Marco's and Nacho's. That is how marriages work."

Tears welled up in Sarah's eyes, and her throat felt thick. She whirled around, striding away from their gate. How could he do that? How could he trust a virtual *stranger* like that? She'd read about these kinds of things happening, people meeting people online, marrying them, then stealing all their money.

She wiped a tear off her cheek as she found an empty gate and took a chair that faced the windows. How could everything have changed so much? How could her dad have let it change?

She dropped her things on the floor and unzipped the small front pocket on her backpack. She pulled out the ziplock of her carry-on liquids and took out the perfume flacon that had been her mom's. She unscrewed the top and held it to her nose, breathing in her mother. She whispered, "I miss you. I miss you so much."

Her dad sat down beside her, and she quickly shoved the perfume back in the ziplock and stuffed it in her backpack. He put a hand on her leg. "Sweetie, I know this is hard. It's hard to move on."

She wiped her nose and said, "You don't seem to be having any trouble."

Her dad sighed.

Sarah kicked her backpack. "It's like you don't even miss Mom."

Her dad leaned forward and put his elbows on his knees, then stared out the window. "I have missed her for six years."

"Then how could you marry someone else?" Sarah sniffled.

"You don't think it was hard for me? To see her get sick and . . ." He trailed off, staring out the window for a moment. "We had so many plans for the three of us. She wanted to take you back to Japan, to show you where she lived when she was little." He shook his head. "For a long time, I could barely function. It was all I could do to go to work, pay the bills." He stared down at his feet for a moment. Then he raised his head and smiled at her. "But I had you to think about. And we got through it, right?"

Sarah nodded. "I thought we were doing fine. I don't get why you have to bring *them* into our life."

"You probably won't understand until you're older.

For now, I guess . . . you have to trust me. Trust that I know what is best for our family." He put an arm around her and she leaned into his shoulder.

She had gotten used to their small family. Being with him, just the two of them, felt right. Why wasn't it enough for him? Sarah let herself pretend it was still just the two of them, that there was not an evil stepmother and her two children waiting for them at Gate 86. Trouble was, pretending wasn't as easy as it used to be. Eventually, she would have to get up and follow her dad, back to their most unwelcome new family. She asked, "But what if this isn't the best thing for our family?"

He patted her arm. "That's what this trip is for. So we can all get to know each other, figure out how this thing is going to work."

And suddenly, just like that, Sarah saw a light at the end of that deep, dark tunnel she'd been heading for. *The trip.* What if it didn't work out? What if all the trip did was prove that the Murillos *were not* the best thing for their family? Maybe she should stop looking at the trip as a drag and look at it as an opportunity: an opportunity to get her life back to the way it was. She sat up and smiled at her dad. "You're right. This will be a great chance to get to know my new brothers. And stepmother."

Her dad looked surprised for a moment, but then he leaned forward and kissed her on the forehead. "That's my girl. Ready to head back to our gate? Start this journey?"

"Oh yeah." Sarah nodded. "I'm more than ready." She got a good grip on her backpack as her dad grabbed the bag from the shop. She followed him, already making plans for how to prove to her dad that the Murillos were the worst thing that could ever happen to her family.

# 4

Seven hours into the fourteen-hour flight to Shanghai, Marco woke up and glanced at his watch. Fifteen minutes? He'd been trying to sleep for seven hours and had only been asleep *fifteen minutes*?

He groaned, not caring who heard him.

The flight was never going to end. And when it did, there would be the ten-hour flight to Australia, and then, finally, the four-hour flight to Fiji.

Marco knew that long before he ever arrived in Fiji, he would be long gone, having succumbed to complications from sheer boredom and discomfort.

On his right, Sarah had fallen asleep wearing her lime-green inflatable neck pillow, but sagged over and landed on Marco's shoulder. He pushed on her head, but it didn't budge.

She responded by snoring.

"Seriously?" When his mother had told him they were sitting separately on the plane, he'd assumed he and his mom and Nacho would be the three and Sarah and her dad the two.

But then Nacho had put up a fuss—which Marco could *tell* was totally fake—about wanting to be next to their mom, and then John had put up a slightly more mature fuss—which Marco could only *suspect* was fake—about it being his honeymoon and wanting to sit by his bride.

Thus, Marco and Sarah had ended up together, seated near the back, in a pair of seats on the side. Marco stared out the window, where he saw nothing but darkness.

Nacho's meltdown had to be bogus, because they'd both been on tons of trips with their mom. Usually they had to fly standby, and sometimes they got to sit up in first class. Marco looked again at Sarah, whose mouth had dropped open, a thin line of drool threatening to escape at any time.

"Oh, no way." Marco shoved Sarah's shoulder, forcing her upright.

Her head jerked, and she blinked. "What?" She sounded groggy. Sarah looked first to her right and then at Marco. She blinked again and wiped her mouth, obviously not entirely awake. Then she frowned, realizing where she was. *And* who she was with. "Why did you wake me up? I finally got to sleep."

"What?" Marco's forehead wrinkled. "You've been sleeping almost the whole flight. And most of the time on me!"

Sarah quickly leaned away from him, stretching her top half out into the aisle. "I was not."

"Oh, *okay*. Whatever. " Giving up on sleep, Marco put his headphones on and tapped the screen of the built-in entertainment monitor on the back of the seat in front of him, hoping for some kind of decent movie.

But the screen stayed dark. "Seriously?"

Sarah noticed him having trouble and tapped her own screen. Nothing. She shrugged and pulled an e-reader out of her bag, then switched on her overhead light.

Marco just sat there, still tapping the screen that obviously was not going to work for him.

Sarah looked at him for a moment, as if trying to decide something, then let out a little sigh. She pulled the Harry Potter from her backpack, and held it out. "Need a book?"

Marco glanced at the illustration on the front and got a strange look on his face, like he smelled bad cheese. "I think I'm a little old for wizards."

She rolled her eyes. "Whatever." She started to put it back, then stopped. "But, just to check, you liked it when you were a kid, right?" When Marco didn't reply, Sarah asked, "You did *read* the books, didn't you?"

Marco shook his head slightly.

Sarah's mouth dropped open. She said, a bit too loudly for a dark plane where everyone was sleeping, "You've never read Harry Potter? Who doesn't read *Harry Potter*?" Then she asked, in a more curious tone, like she really wanted to know, "How have you never read Harry Potter?"

Marco scowled. "I don't like to read."

Sarah rolled her eyes. "Oh, but you saw the movies right? Of course you did." She shook her head. "Didn't read the books, but saw the movies." She clicked her tongue a couple times. "What a cliché."

Marco adjusted himself in order to face her more squarely. "For your information, no, I have not seen the movies either."

Sarah's mouth, again, dropped open a bit. And again, she said, much too loudly for a dark plane where everyone was sleeping, "You've never seen the movies? How have you never seen the movies?"

"Shh!" Marco held a finger to his lips. "You are so loud." He sighed. "I'm not a big reader, so I didn't read the books. And . . ." He didn't say anything else.

She rolled her eyes. "Oh, I need to know this." Sarah prodded him. "And what?"

He faced forward again. He didn't really want to admit what he was going to admit, but he knew it was the only way to get his snoopy stepsister/seatmate off his back. He said, "My mom wouldn't let me see the movies without reading the books first. And so I thought, what's the big deal anyway? But then all my friends were into the movies, and I didn't think I could sit and read all seven books so I could watch the movies and . . . I just pretended like I didn't care."

Sarah's eyes were wide, listening like she'd never heard something so unbelievable in her life. "Why didn't you give in and read them?"

Marco shrugged. "It just became more important to stand my ground, not read the books. And not see the movies."

Sarah held the book up, waving it a little bit. "But you want to, right? Don't you feel left out? Don't you want to know what *everyone else in the civilized world* knows?"

She didn't sound mean, she just sounded like she was on a mission to get him to do something he didn't really want to do. Marco looked out the window at the dark nothingness.

Sarah nudged him with her elbow. "You have to read it."

Marco looked at her. "Why?"

She shrugged. "Because . . . they are the best and you are totally missing out?" Sarah waggled the volume in her hand. "I've read this eleven times. And I dragged it along to read again."

Marco looked at the book. "It's pretty thick."

Sarah shoved it at him, not all that unkindly. "Trust me, it'll fly by and you'll be reading 'The End' before you know it. And then you'll be hooked and want to read the next one. Guarantee it." Pompously, she tapped her e-reader. "Got them all on here. And then when you're done, you can watch all the movies, which, by the way, I own on DVD."

There was nothing for Marco to do on that flight but sit there and not sleep and not watch a movie on the entertainment screen that did not work. So he reached up and pushed the button for the overhead light. He took ahold of the book, which he had no intention of even opening.

# 5

Sarah scrunched up her nose against the musty smell and took one lengthy and disgusted look at the hotel room. Threadbare bedspread. Yellowed pillowcases. Warped and dirty wooden headboard.

As exhausted as she was, after being on planes and dragging through airports for the past thirty-five hours, she could not picture herself lying on that bed. She could not even picture herself touching anything in that heinous hotel room. The only bright spot was that making the trip seem bad was going to be simpler than she planned, and she didn't even have to act her way through this situation.

She spun on her heel and headed back out to the hallway. "No way, not doing it. I'll probably catch bed-bugs. Or some rare tropical disease."

Her father had dark bags under his eyes and looked to be in no mood for any nonsense. "Sarah, it's just for one night. We go on our cruise tomorrow."

Sarah scowled. "If it's just for one night, then why are we in a dive?"

Her father blew out a long breath. "The resort wouldn't let the five of us stay in the room I reserved for two. Despite the fact it was a suite with a pullout couch." He held out his hands. "This one didn't seem that bad. We don't really have any other options at the last minute. It's this or the street. And I am tired."

Sarah was rather confident that the street would be nicer, but she kept her opinion to herself.

Yvonna came down the hallway, rolling her suitcase, the boys following behind. She said, "Sarah, I'll stay with you and let your dad and the boys share the other room."

Sleep with her stepmother? No way! Sarah opened her mouth to protest, but her dad shot a dark look her way. She shut her mouth.

Yvonna stepped into the doorway and froze, then sucked her lower lip inside her mouth.

John let out an exasperated sigh. "I know, I know, it's fairly sketchy. But we have no choice."

Yvonna set a hand on his arm. "It'll be fine." She

smiled at her boys. "Inconvenience is adventure, wrongly considered. Right? And it's just for one night."

Marco and Nacho exchanged a glance. Nacho unzipped his fanny pack, took out a clear travel-size bottle of hand sanitizer, and squeezed out a large dollop onto his palm, the stark smell of alcohol drifting toward Sarah. Then he held the bottle up and Marco held out his hand for some.

Marco rubbed his hands together. "We've stayed in worse."

Sarah shook her head and went back inside the room. There was only the one bed, and it was a smallish queen size. Really? She had to actually sleep with her new stepmother?

Things could not possibly get any worse.

She dropped her suitcase and unzipped it to grab her bag of toiletries, and went into the dark bathroom.

Sarah flipped the switch, flooding the windowless room with light.

A cockroach the size of her thumb skittered across the floor.

Her scream was a high-pitched sound that pierced the middle-of-the-night quiet and brought the other four running. Sarah pointed to the toilet. "A huge cockroach! He went behind there!"

"Probably a palmetto bug," said John. "He won't bother you."

Marco said, "Unless they fly like they do in Texas."

Sarah glared at him.

Yvonna held out a key. "Good *night*, Marco."

He took the key and hauled his suitcase to the door across the hall. He opened it and disappeared inside, Nacho right on his heels.

John said, "Keep the light on in here and the bug won't come back."

Sarah looked out into the room. If that was the case, those lights were not going off, ever. She did not want to wake up in the dark and find one of those—she shuddered—*things* crawling on her.

"I want to go home!" She slammed the bathroom door and unzipped her bag. As she did her nightly ritual of flossing and brushing, she kept stealing glances at the toilet, waiting for that unspeakable *nasty* to make another unwanted appearance. When she finished in there, without seeing anything worse than the grungy tile floor, she went back out into the room.

Her father had gone, and Yvonna sat on the edge of the bed. She yawned. Her eyes were a little bloodshot and she looked tired. "All done in there?"

On the flight, Sarah had decided giving Yvonna the silent treatment might be one way to ruin the trip, but she couldn't help responding. "It's *so* disgusting."

Yvonna took a glance around. "I'm sure you're used to staying in better hotels than this." She handed a brochure to Sarah. "Your dad left this for you. Thought it might be reassuring for you to see what our sailing cruise will be like."

Sarah didn't make any move to take it from her, so Yvonna set it on the bed, went into the bathroom, and closed the door.

Sarah leapt at the bed and snatched up the brochure, which proclaimed:

The photograph on the front was of a large, pristine wooden sailboat with crisp white sails, afloat a gorgeous crystal-blue sea. She opened the brochure and started reading:

This sixty-foot vessel provides luxury charters, skippered by an internationally experienced captain with a wealth of local knowledge. In addition, private cruises include a fully qualified chef, whose culinary talents indulge guests with gourmet meals prepared fresh with local ingredients. Even the fussiest of taste buds will succumb to the delightful fare.

Sounded good so far.

Enjoy visiting unspoiled bays, picturesque harbors, and uninhabited atolls accessible only by boat. Ends of the Earth will get you to the ends of the earth . . . in one-of-a-kind, luxurious style.

"Nice." Sarah grinned. "That's way more of what I'm used to."

Then she got into bed, cringing at the sandpapery sheets. She lay on her side, hugging the edge, then stuck one of the two pillows from her side right behind her back. A wall between her and her new stepmother. Sarah closed her eyes and pretended to be asleep, awash with relief that the sailboat would be a thousand times better than the hotel room.

# 6

The next morning they crowded into a taxi that took them to the harbor. After they unloaded, Marco stood at the dock, shaking his head at the vessel that floated in front of them. "That's it?" The sailboat, if it could be called that, was about sixty feet long. The white paint was peeling off in spots, revealing bare wood underneath. The sails were nearly all furled, but the slim strip of material visible to Marco seemed dingy, not bright white like he had anticipated. The lines tying the sailboat to the mooring were so frayed they looked like a good yank would break them in half. A faded sign, a bit off-kilter, declared HMS *MOONFLIGHT.*

He stepped closer to the boat and looked down into the water. On the hull, below the water line, was a brown film, with some seaweedy, grassy parts in spots. Marco wrinkled his nose. That couldn't be good.

"Is this thing safe?" Nacho was already paging through the "Boating Safety" chapter in his Eco-Scout manual. "Because it does *not* look all that safe to me."

Sarah let loose with a near growl. "You've got to be kidding me!" She dug around in her bag, and then brandished a shiny brochure. "That's not the boat!"

John took the brochure and looked at it, then back at the sailboat. "Actually . . ." He squinted at the sailboat. "Add a new coat of paint and some new sails, and . . . I think it *is* this boat."

Sarah grabbed the brochure back and glared at it. "How many decades ago was that picture even taken? This is such false advertising." Turning her back to him, she crossed her arms, staring out at the harbor. "How could you not check it out before we got here?"

Actually, Marco found himself wondering the same thing.

A man with a shock of white hair on his head and a few days' of gray, bristly beard on his face jumped off the *Moonflight* and onto the dock. Thin and muscular, he wore blue board shorts and a grungy white T-shirt with a small hole near the bottom hem. He took off his navy-blue captain's hat and bowed his head slightly.

"Welcome to *Moonflight*. I'm Captain Norm."

John held out his hand and shook. "Um, thanks. I'm not sure we're in the right place." He pointed at the brochure in Sarah's hand. "We booked the luxury cruise?"

Captain Norm grinned, revealing a couple of gold teeth. Quickly, he pivoted around and pointed at his back with the index fingers of both hands. Everyone read the words on the back of his T-shirt:

Facing them again, he held both his arms out straight. "This is the place!"

"Oh man," mumbled Marco. What were they getting into?

Yvonna pulled on John's arm. "Are you sure this is the cruise you booked? I expected something . . . nicer."

Sarah narrowed her eyes and spat out, "What, this boat isn't good enough for you?" Then Sarah dragged her suitcase toward *Moonflight*.

Nacho followed.

John called out, "Hey, kids. I'm not so sure about this. Hold on a sec—"

Captain Norm tilted his head at John. "Is there a problem?" His tone was slightly threatening.

Angry at Sarah for making his mom seem like a diva when she most certainly wasn't, Marco scowled as he watched his new stepfather retreat a bit.

John said, "I'm not sure this is the kind of vessel we were planning on boarding."

Captain Norm crossed his arms and his thick, bushy eyebrows knotted together. "Something wrong with my boat?"

John shook his head. "No, no, I didn't mean anything like that."

Marco rolled his eyes. Of course John would back down. Distaste for his new stepfather swam in his head. Marco scoffed, "What, scared of a stupid boat?" And he picked up his duffel bag and headed for the sailboat.

Yvonna and John exchanged a glance, a lengthy one loaded with exhaustion, desperation, and a tad bit of defeat. John sighed. "Fine. Let's just load up."

On board, a slim, well-muscled young man with bleached blond hair that contrasted with his darkly tanned skin took their luggage downstairs. Captain

Norm directed everyone to an open area at the back of the boat where a few dented lawn chairs sat haphazardly. "Have a seat. I have to deal with the inspector."

The family sat and watched as a sunburned, portly man with a clipboard stepped on board. He took a cursory look around the boat before asking Norm, "You're the skipper?"

Captain Norm nodded.

"First mate? You know a boat this size needs a crew of two around here." The inspector looked around. "You're not putting anything past me, are you?"

Marco and Nacho exchanged a glance.

Captain Norm grinned. "Of course not." He whistled, and the young man came bounding up the stairs and handed a piece of paper to the inspector. The inspector nodded. "First mate, Ahab . . . I can't read the last name?"

"My penmanship isn't what it used to be." Captain Norm reached out to grab the sheet of paper, but the inspector waved him away. "No matter. Ahab is good enough. What matters is you've actually *got* a first mate." He walked around a bit more, and then disembarked.

Captain Norm called out, "All aboard that's goin' aboard!"

"We're already here," Marco muttered. He had

been hoping the boat wouldn't pass inspection. No such luck.

The skipper called out to John, "Can you get the bowline for me?"

John stepped out onto the dock and stood there, looking around.

Captain Norm pointed to the front of the boat. John undid the line, tossed it onto the boat, and then stepped back on. The young man did the same thing to the line at the back of the boat, then leapt aboard.

As the motor started up and the boat began to pull away from the dock, Marco felt his heart speed up. He'd never been on a boat on the open ocean, and he was excited. He and Nacho went up to the front of the boat, where the fresh, salty breeze blew into their faces, a bit of refreshing sea spray with it.

Marco rode backward to watch the sails unfurl. They were a dull white, with dark, patchy parts. Mold, maybe? He was relieved to see no holes, though, and turned back around as *Moonflight* headed out. As the boat reached the harbor's mouth, just as they were about to enter the open sea—

*Kerploosh!*

Marco and Nacho ran to the side of the boat and leaned over the railing, looking back toward shore and the sound of the splash. No one had surfaced yet. Marco crossed his fingers, hoping either John or Sarah had fallen overboard, never to be seen again. But as they watched, a bleached-blond head poked out of the waves while strong, tanned arms began to confidently stroke their way back toward the dock.

"Hey!" yelled Nacho, pointing at the swimmer. "Ahab is going back to shore!"

Captain Norm, at the helm, called, "Naw, he's not." Then he whistled, a different tone from before, and from down below scampered up what looked like a smallish bear, but what was actually an enormous black Newfoundland.

Sarah screeched as the dog put its giant paws up into her lap and began licking her face.

Captain Norm laughed. "*That* is Ahab."

"Our first mate is a dog?" Nacho opened his Eco-Scouts manual. "That does *not* seem safe to me. Not at all." He paged through a bit, shaking his head. "I'm pretty sure that's not even allowed."

Sarah fell over in her chair, shrieking, the dog on top of her as John tried to pull him back. Marco leaned back against the railing and laughed. The trip might not be that bad after all.

# 7

Sarah was on her knees, head sticking out between the strands of rope railing, heaving her guts into the wake of the sailboat. Her head swirled and she just wanted to lie down. But as soon as her head hit the deck, the next dip of the boat had her nausea surging, and she was back up on her knees in seconds. The boat leaned from side to side, as if it were going to tip over, making her scared as well as sick. "Dad, I want to get off!"

"Sarah, I am so sorry." John paced the deck behind her. "I never even thought of bringing motion sickness pills. I never get sick on boats; your mother never got sick on boats." He stepped over to the hatch and yelled down into it. "Did you find anything yet?"

Captain Norm came up from below and stepped

back onto the deck, holding a small white bottle. "Found some."

John sighed and took the bottle. "Oh, thank goodness." He glanced at the label and frowned. "These expired three years ago."

Captain Norm shrugged. "They only put expiration dates on those things so you'll buy more. I'm sure they're fine."

John shook his head and handed them back. "You can keep them."

"Dad," Sarah moaned. "Do something." She lay down on her side, both hands curled under her head. She shut her eyes, but then the motion seemed worse.

Yvonna came up the stairs. "I made some ginger tea. Well, not exactly tea, just sugar and ginger, but it might make you feel better. I give it to the boys when they have sore throats."

Sarah glared at her. "My throat is fine."

Yvonna nodded. "I know. But some people also swear it's a cure for seasickness. Want to try?"

"Thanks," said John. He took the mug and knelt by Sarah. "Honey? Want to try this?"

Sarah did not want to take anything from Yvonna, but she was desperate, not dumb. If there was the slightest chance that the tea would stop the rolling in her head . . .

She nodded.

Her dad helped her sit up and held on to her back as she took a cautious sip. She made a face. "It's like . . . spicy. But not." She took another sip, then held the mug in both her hands, letting the steam curl up into her face. She breathed in, liking the smell. "I'll drink it." Although she still felt like her head was about to fall off, the tea gave her something to think about besides being sick. She faced the front of the ship, trying to focus on the horizon, which was the only thing not moving as far as she could tell.

Ahab came and lay down beside her, snout on his outstretched paws. Sarah thought he looked meek and apologetic, almost as if he felt it were his fault for her being sick. Despite his overzealous greeting earlier, Sarah found it hard to hold a grudge, so she set her hand on his hefty back and rubbed. "Hey, boy." He wore a navy blue collar with a silver anchor-shaped tag. Sarah held it so she could read the word on it. AHABB. "I thought it was spelled with only one *B*."

"It is." Captain Norm stopped and patted the dog's head. "Dumb company misspelled his name. He had a better tag, but he lost it on an island last year." He scratched his chin. "In fact, I think he lost it on the island we're heading to."

"Maybe we'll find it," said Sarah.

Captain Norm smiled. "Maybe." He tipped back his hat and pointed out at the water. "See anything interesting?"

"Like what?"

Captain Norm rubbed his bristled chin. "You never know. Dolphins. Whales. Mermaids."

Sarah smirked. "Okay, I'll keep an eye out for mermaids."

The skipper narrowed his eyes. "I'm serious." He looked out at the waves. "I've been sailing since I was eighteen. Spent seven years in the Caribbean." He raised his eyebrows at Sarah. "Met some interesting folks."

"Mermaids?" Sarah rolled her eyes.

He pointed at her. "I met people who believed in them. Old men who had been on the seas for years. They had stories. They believed."

Sarah frowned. "Do you believe in mermaids?"

Captain Norm grinned. "If you'd seen some of the things I've seen? You'd believe in just about anything." He stood and headed back to the helm.

Nacho followed him, holding his Eco-Scout safety

manual out in front of him. He asked, "How many personal flotation devices do you have on board? You need to have at least one for each passenger."

Captain Norm pointed to the back of the boat, near Sarah and Ahab. "Check the locker there."

Nacho went to the back. He wrapped his hand in the bottom of his T-shirt and lifted the creaky lid of the wooden locker. A strong, musty odor wafted out and Nacho made a face. He pulled out a misshapen, drab orange life jacket that was lumpier in some spots than others. He held the strap by two fingers, protected by the bottom of his shirt.

Sarah said, "That looks a thousand years old."

Nacho leaned forward and looked into the locker, and his lips moved silently as he counted. "There's enough for all of us."

"Disgusting." Sarah shook her head. "I'm not wearing one."

Her dad said, "You wouldn't be so picky in an emergency."

Sarah shivered. "Can we not talk about it?" She took another sip of ginger tea.

Nacho set the life jacket on the deck in the bright sun and started pulling out the others. "Maybe airing them out will help." After he had lined up the six life jackets, he pulled a bottle of hand sanitizer out of his fanny pack and drenched his hands. Then he opened up his manual and paged through. He called to Captain Norm, "Did you file a float plan?"

Captain Norm nodded.

Sarah asked, "What's that?"

Nacho said, "It tells where you're going, when you'll be back. In case something happens, someone will know where to look for you."

Sarah looked around and saw nothing but ocean and a few distant islands. "How could anyone find anyone in this?"

"GPS," replied Nacho. "It's not as hard as you think as long as you have some coordinates to start with."

John asked Captain Norm, "Where exactly are we headed?"

Captain Norm pointed straight ahead. "There's a nice private island about a day's sail from here. I haven't been there for a while, but I think it'll be perfect for you all. We'll anchor and spend three days, then head back." He glanced up at the cloudless sky. "If this breeze holds through the night, we should make it there about dawn tomorrow."

As Sarah looked out onto the endless stretch of water, a large white bird with turquoise feet circled the boat. Sarah stared, noticing the bird's yellow eyes. "What is that?"

Captain Norm called out, "Blue-footed booby."

Marco laughed.

Sarah rolled her eyes. "Real mature."

"It's a funny name." Marco narrowed his eyes at her. "I just meant that there's no way there's a bird called that."

As they watched, the bird sped like a missile toward the water and dove, surfacing a moment later with a fish in its mouth.

"Whoa!" Nacho whooped. "That was cool."

Captain Norm said, "The blue-footed booby's nostrils are permanently closed because they dive so much. But there's also the masked booby, the brown booby, and the red-footed booby." Captain Norm looked at Marco and tilted his head. "See for yourself. There's a bird book down in the hold."

Sarah said, "That would require knowing how to read." And then she felt a surge of nausea and leaned out over the rail, too busy puking to notice the scathing look that Marco shot her way.

# 8

Marco pushed open the hatch and stomped down the few stairs into the cabin, more to get away from everyone than to look for the stupid book about the stupid birds who lived on the stupid ocean. He sighed, and wished he were back in Texas with his friends. The light coming through the portholes was enough to see by as he got his first look at the space belowdecks.

His eyes widened.

The cabin was in much less disrepair than the rest of the boat, and actually looked habitable. Even rather nice, despite the slight musty odor. The front of the boat made a V, where there was a berth, the bed neatly made with a blue spread and a white pillow. He hoped that he could sleep there, although he suspected he would end up sharing with Nacho.

The galley was small, but seemed to have all the amenities of a regular kitchen. A large wooden basket of fresh pineapples, papayas, and tiny bananas sat on the counter, tethered by the handle with a red-and-black bungee cord. Just past the kitchen a red-and-white-checked tablecloth covered a rectangular table, which was bolted to the wall at one end, a green-cushioned banquette curving around three sides of it. A few steps beyond the table lay a sitting room, with two wide cushioned built-in benches that met in one corner and lay opposite a shelving unit that held a television.

Marco smiled. "Nice." He stepped closer and pushed the power button, but nothing happened. He hoped there was nothing wrong with the television, that it just happened to be unplugged or something.

Several bookshelves sat above the television, and Marco stepped over to read the spines of the books. He half hoped to find another in the Harry Potter series, since he'd devoured the first during the flight from Shanghai to Sydney while everyone else slept. When they'd landed, he handed it to Sarah, with a flip, "I won't need this after all," implying that he hadn't even cracked it open.

He wasn't exactly sure why, but he just didn't want her to know he'd read it. Maybe he didn't want to be a source of satisfaction for her; she'd made him feel like he was some kind of project.

He was getting the feeling that the trip was like a test of some sort for the Robinsons, to see if this new *family* was going to work. So far, really, it couldn't have been going any worse. Between the long flights, the lousy hotel, the suckfest of a boat . . . He grinned. The trip couldn't have been going any better, because the worse it went, the better chance there was that his new stepfather—and maybe even his mom—would give up on the marriage. And they'd end up back in Texas.

He perused the bookshelf, which held a dozen or so old, mildewed books, by authors with odd names like Jules Verne and Homer and H. G. Wells and Robert Louis Stevenson, but no Harry Potter. He found the bird book and pulled it out.

Marco peered into the small head, surprised to see sparkling silver metal fixtures on the sink and toilet, and clean white tile. "Mom will be happy about that." On his way back to the galley, he noticed a small table and chair he hadn't seen before, with a bank of electronics above them. A headset lay on the table, and he picked it up and put it on. "Mayday, Mayday." He grinned. Then he took off the headset and set it back on the table.

On his way back out, he passed a door with a sign that read CREW ONLY.

Marco went over to the foot of the stairs, peered up, and then backed his way to the door. He took ahold of the knob, expecting it to be locked, but it twisted easily in his hand and he pushed the door open.

The berth wasn't very large, and held only a desk, a chair, and a bed, neatly made with a white bedspread decorated with a stitched dark blue anchor. At the foot of the bed sat a square object, concealed completely by a plain white sheet.

Marco leaned back out the door for a second, checking to see that no one had come down the stairs, then quickly stepped to the end of the bed. He lifted one end of the white sheet, revealing a large trunk made of a dark wood, intricately carved scenes all over it. He saw mermaids and islands and even what looked like a sea monster. Each of the carvings was inlaid with colorful abalone, and Marco couldn't resist touching one. The shiny surface was smooth and cool under his fingertips.

The latch for the trunk was closed, and Marco

pressed his fingers against the mechanism, trying to spring it open.

Nothing happened.

"Marco?" His mother's voice came from above.

He dropped the corner of the sheet, backed out of the room, and shut the door. "Coming!" Then, clutching the bird book in his hand, he headed up to the deck.

# 9

By the time the sun was almost ready to kiss the horizon, Sarah had gotten over the worst of her nausea. While she certainly wasn't about to give credit for the improvement to the ginger tea, and especially not her stepmother, she was grateful to be feeling better.

Sarah and Ahab perched near the front of the boat as it sailed east, away from the sunset. Captain Norm was at the helm, eating his dinner, while the others were down in the cabin eating theirs.

Apparently, their captain fit the brochure description of *fully qualified chef,* because he had slipped away from steering the boat about an hour before, then reappeared, proclaiming, "Soup's on!"

Although she was feeling better, the thought of

eating—even simply smelling food—was enough to make her gag, and she stayed above while the others descended to eat whatever gourmet meal awaited them. The ocean breeze felt good on her face, gradually cooling as the sun slipped below the waves. The first star appeared in the twilight, joined by others, rapidly multiplying as the sky darkened. The moon, half full, began creeping up the sky.

Sarah lay back on a towel and stared up at the constellations. Her dad had shown her a few on last summer's trip to the Caribbean, but she only remembered one. She held her hand up toward the sky, tracing the lines of the Southern Cross.

Ahab barked.

She looked at him. "What's a matter—" Then Sarah looked back up at the sky and froze.

The stars had vanished. As had the moon.

Ahab barked again.

Sarah sat up. Seconds before she had seen no clouds at all, but the stars were now . . . gone. How was that possible?

Captain Norm's face was visible in the green glow of the control panel. He stood there, not moving, staring up at the sky.

Ahab barked and barked, not stopping.

Over the din, Sarah asked, "What happened?"

Captain Norm shook his head. "I think we've run into some weather."

The breeze picked up. Sarah set her hand on Ahab's head, but he wouldn't stop barking.

Captain Norm said, "I don't like the looks of this."

Sarah stood up, almost losing her balance after sitting for so long. "Is it a storm?"

"Probably just a squall. You should go down in the cabin." He took a long look at Ahab. "Take my dog with you. I'm going to furl the sail and turn on the autopilot. Can you send your dad up? I'll need a hand with the sail."

Although she barely knew him, the tone in his voice was not to be argued with, so Sarah didn't even consider disobeying. She pulled on Ahab's collar, dragging him. Not an easy task, as he kept barking and looking back at the captain.

When they reached the hatch, Sarah said, "Come on. We have to get below."

But Ahab grew quiet and sat back on his haunches. He looked over at his master and began whining.

Captain Norm called over, "Go on, Ahab. Go on."

Sarah forced herself to sound calm. "Come on, boy. It's just a storm. We'll be fine." Even as the reassuring words came out of her mouth, her heart raced and her hands trembled as they grasped the dog's thick collar. She didn't know how bad the storm would be. She didn't know if they would be fine. But she did know she needed to get that dog downstairs.

She set a hand on his massive head and his brown eyes gazed up at her.

"I promise. I'll take good care of you."

Ahab took one last look at Captain Norm, then got to his feet and headed down the stairs into the cabin. Before she followed, she glanced over at the captain. He was hunched over his controls, speaking into his handheld radio.

We'll be fine, thought Sarah. He was already calling for help and nothing bad had even happened.

Just as she began to step down, a draft lifted her hair off her shoulders. And then, as the breeze stiffened into a wind, rain began pelting her face. She quickly took the stairs down into the cabin, and burst into the galley.

Ahab paced back and forth in the small space, his tail low, not wagging in the slightest.

Everyone else was seated in the booth, eating spaghetti from the looks of Nacho, whose chin was utterly orange.

John smiled. "Hungry?"

Sarah shook her head as she wiped rain off her face. "A storm's coming."

Yvonna frowned. "But the sky was so clear."

"Not anymore," said Sarah, surprised at herself that there was not a trace of snark in her words. She was too puzzled by how fast the storm had come up. "The stars disappeared and Captain Norm sent us down here."

Her dad stood up. "I wonder if he needs help."

Sarah said, "He wants us to stay down here."

The captain hadn't used those words *exactly*, but something inside Sarah told her she needed to keep her family downstairs. Well, her dad was her only family, really, but she didn't want anything to happen to anyone on that boat. So a little white lie wasn't going to hurt if it did, in fact, keep them all safe inside the cabin.

The boat began to rock, and then, suddenly, the dishes on the table slid to one side.

"Grab them!" yelled Yvonna.

Luckily, the edge of the table had a lip that stopped the dishes before the boys had a chance to react. Sarah picked up the pot of noodles and sauce. Together they quickly piled dirty dishes in the small sink and everything else in the cupboard above the sink, firmly securing the latch on the cabinet.

Sarah realized she'd better tell her dad the captain

needed help. "Dad, I forgot. The captain wanted you to help him with the sail."

John quickly headed up on deck.

By the time they were done cleaning up the dinner table, the thunder and wind and rain were so loud that they had to yell to be heard. The boat was all over the place, climbing up and then plunging so far that Sarah's stomach lurched like she was on a roller coaster.

Her dad came back down.

Yvonna asked, "What's going on?"

John said, "We got the sail put away and the skipper put the boat on autopilot." He tried to smile. "Let's go in and sit down."

Grabbing at the knobs on the cupboard and then the table in order to keep her balance, Sarah followed him into the other small room and they all crowded together on the cushioned benches, no one saying anything. Sarah's heart was pounding and she felt like she had to throw up again. Her dad put his arm around her. "You okay?"

She wanted to scream. She wanted so badly to stand up and shout, *"No, I'm not okay! I want to be home! With you and me, the way it was!"* If it weren't for the Murillo three that is exactly where they would be. Safe and sound in Southern California.

But instead of saying any of what she was really feeling, she chose to share only a small part of it. She said, "I don't like this."

But no one answered her, because a second after the words came out, the lights in the cabin went out. They were in the belly of the sailboat, in the dark, in the middle of a maelstrom.

And then, finally, Sarah did let out the scream she had been holding in.

# 10

Marco was unsure whether he hit the floor before or after the lights went off, but either way, he found himself in complete blackness, face to floor, his nose buried in the musty rug. He scrambled up onto all fours, reaching out with one hand for something to steady himself with as the boat pitched violently to the side. He called out, "Mom!"

"Marco!"

His mom sounded very close, so he reached out. His fingers brushed an arm, so he grasped and held on, pulling.

"Dad?" The voice attached to the arm was tearful. And girly.

Marco quickly let go of Sarah. "I'm not your dad."

"Marco!"

A hand gripped his shoulder and he quickly grabbed it. "Mom?"

"Yes, it's me, sweetie." Her voice was shaky. "I have Nacho's hand. John?"

John answered, "I have Sarah! Yvonna, where's your hand?"

Marco heard a crash as something fell. His mom sounded frantic as she asked, "Do we have everyone?"

John said, "I think so. I saw a flashlight in the kitchen, you all stay right here."

The storm had increased in intensity and Marco could hear only the howling wind and rain driving against the boat, which all the while rocked violently from side to side as the front rose up, up, up—then dropped, forcing Marco to let go of his mom.

"Hold on!" John yelled. "Just grab something!"

Someone grabbed Marco's arm and he had no idea who it was. Did it even matter?

Suddenly a beam of light blinded him.

"You all okay?"

Marco held a hand over his eyes as they adjusted to the light. John held on to the built-in shelf with one hand, the flashlight in his other one. Marco looked around. Yvonna, her eyes wide and face pale, had one arm around

Nacho and the other around Sarah, both of whom were crying. Nacho had Marco's arm, and Ahab was seated right next to Sarah, licking tears off her face.

Marco looked back at John. "What do we do?"

"Only thing we *can* do," said John. "Ride this storm out." As his eyes darted around the interior of the boat, the smile on his face appeared utterly false.

Marco swallowed. His heartbeat sped up. He could tell by the look on John's face exactly what he was thinking: His stepfather was worried about the boat itself surviving the storm.

Taking a few uneven steps at a time, John slowly made his way to Sarah and set his hand on her head before placing a hand on his wife's shoulder. He knelt by Nacho and leaned down by his ear. He said something, but Marco couldn't tell what it was. Nacho wiped his nose and nodded, then told John something. John smiled and set a hand on Nacho's head, then stood back up.

He went into the closest bedroom. The glow of the flashlight flitted around, and then John returned holding a lantern. He switched it on, instantly brightening the room while throwing shadows about. Then he said, "You all stay here, I'll be back."

Sarah called out, "Dad!"

Yvonna started to say something, but John held up a hand. "Stay here. I'll be right back."

Marco watched him head through the kitchen. He quickly got to his feet and began to follow.

"Marco!" yelled his mom. "You stay here!"

Marco nodded. "I'm just going into the galley." But when he got into the galley, it was empty. Had John gone up the stairs into the storm? Was he crazy? Marco pulled out a kitchen drawer, hoping for another flashlight. Nothing. He checked another one.

"Yes!" He grabbed it and clicked it on. The boat may have been a piece of crap, but apparently the skipper spared no expense when it came to flashlights.

Clutching the edges of the counter, Marco moved to the bottom of the stairs and shone the light at the top. He glanced behind him, then carefully gripped the handrail and, despite losing his balance every time the boat rocked, he made his way up. He pushed on the hatch. The wind pushed back, and he had to put his shoulder against it, all of his weight with him, in order to get it to budge.

As soon as it opened, his face was whipped with drenching gusts of rain and seawater, which stole his breath. He didn't see the sail anymore, and there was a slight green glow from the helm, where the captain was hunched over the instrument panel. Marco swung his flashlight around and the beam let him catch a glimpse of a white face.

"John!" he screamed, his words lost in the wind. What was his new stepfather doing?

John must have heard, or else seen the flashlight's glow, because he looked over at Marco. With one arm, he held on to the rigging for dear life, while in his other hand he held a rope.

Marco wiped the water out of his eyes. What was he doing with—? And then his gaze went to the end of the rope and saw orange. Life jackets. John had come up to get the life jackets.

Ignoring the pounding of his heart, Marco stuck the flashlight in the deep pocket of his board shorts, and the beam shone straight up. With one hand he grasped the hatch, and then he stretched himself out to get as far as he could. The pitch of the boat kept throwing him off balance so that he could barely stay on his feet. *Why do I have to?*

He dropped to his knees. Immediately, he felt much steadier, and much less likely to get blown away. John followed suit. He dropped down and began to crawl toward Marco, one hand gripping the rope with all the life jackets. The boat hit the top of a crest and dove, sending John surging toward Marco.

Marco reached out and grabbed John's arm, pulling him toward the hatch and the stairs. John managed to get a grip on the hatch and rest for a moment. He looked drenched and out of breath, but he yelled at Marco, "Get inside!"

Marco faced inside and went down a few stairs, but held out his hand for John to grab on to. Instead, John handed him the rope with the life jackets. "Get those down!"

Marco grabbed the rope and yanked hard. Then he yanked again, harder, and the tethered life jackets slid partway down the stairs. With that hand free once again, Marco held out his hand to John. "Come on!"

John took the hand and let Marco pull him inside. John shut the hatch and stood there, panting and dripping. Marco headed down the stairs, kicking the life jackets ahead of him as he descended, John right behind him. When they reached the bottom, John said, "Thank you. I don't know if I would have made it."

Marco nodded, too out of breath to say anything.

Together, they took the life jackets in to the others. Sarah's eyes widened as she saw them. "Why do we need those?"

John said, "Just to be safe."

Yvonna said, "It's good to have them just in case.

We don't need to put them on." She glanced up at John. "Right?"

John scratched his chin. "I think we should put them on."

"What?" Sarah looked up at her dad.

Marco said, "It's bad out there."

Yvonna narrowed her eyes at John. "What were you thinking taking my son out there?"

"Mom!" said Marco. "He didn't know. I followed him."

"And it's a good thing he did," said John. "Now let's put these on."

# 11

Sarah tried to stop crying, but she couldn't help it. Ever since the lights went out and she'd had to put on that sodden, stinky life jacket, she just gave up and sat there on the cabin floor, wiping her nose and sniffling.

The day, to put it lightly, had been a disaster all around. First she had spent most of it dizzy, nauseated, and throwing up, and now it seemed she was doomed to spend the rest of it huddled on the floor of a shuddering sailboat in the middle of a horrific storm, waiting for one final blow to send them all to the bottom of the abyss.

The thought brought fresh tears, which crumpled her face and caused her dad to remark, "Sweetie, are you okay?"

Sarah scrunched her eyes shut and shook her head. "I just want the boat to stop moving!"

John put an arm around her and crushed her face into his smelly life jacket. "We'll make it through this," he said. "The storm has to end at some point. And I'm sure the skipper knows what he's doing up there."

Sarah thought her dad did not seem the least bit convinced. His words, despite brimming with reassurance, did nothing to comfort her. She wrapped her arms around her knees and wished to stop moving, to be still. Sarah held her breath, willed her body to freeze, but the boat itself wouldn't stop the constant motion. Even if she stopped her own trembling, the boat refused to do the same.

Yvonna's voice was shaky as she asked, "How long do you think it'll last?"

John shook his head. "I have no idea. I don't get how we could go from clear skies to this so quickly."

Sarah wouldn't have believed it if she hadn't seen it herself. The stars had been there above her, the sky full of them, and then they'd just blinked away.

Ahab nudged her arms and she lifted one, letting him snuggle up to her. His warm body felt comforting, and she put an arm around him. "It's okay, boy."

Nacho sniffled and wiped his eyes. "Maybe we should try and go to sleep."

Yvonna ruffled his hair. "Are you tired?"

Nacho shook his head. "I was hoping I could go to sleep and it would be all over. Like when there's a tornado watch at home, and you tuck me in the sofa bed in the basement, and when I wake up, it's all over."

Marco snorted. "You sleep through everything."

But to Sarah, Marco sounded like he wanted that storm to be over as much as everyone else did. Maybe it was just easier to make fun of his brother than admit he agreed with him.

The sailboat lurched, more violently than before, and Sarah called out, "Dad!"

But John was staggering from one side of the galley to the other as the boat jerked, and then he started up the steps.

Yvonna yelled, "You can't go up there!"

John stopped, took a deep breath, and then faced her. "What if he needs help?"

Sarah stood up, wobbling with the sway of the boat, and then dug her hands gently into Ahab's fur. He led her to the galley. "Dad! Don't go."

"I have to see if there's something I can do to help

save . . ." Then he pushed on the door to the deck. He twisted back around. "Marco, can you help? It's jammed."

Marco climbed the few steps to the hatch and stood beside him. Together, they pushed and managed to open it a bit before it slammed shut. John said, "The wind is too strong! We have to try again."

Suddenly, there was a loud *CRACK* and something slammed hard above them, causing the boat to shudder momentarily.

"Dad!"

Ahab was on his feet, barking at the hatch, trying to get past John, who glanced back at Sarah, before shoving his body into the door. "We've got to get this open!"

Marco stood beside him and they managed to get the door open. John slid through and was gone, Ahab at his heels, a burst of seawater pouring in where they stood as the door slammed shut.

*I have to see if there's something I can do to save . . .*

Sarah hadn't heard the end of his sentence. But she could imagine what he said, and she filled in the last few words. . . . *the boat. Us.*

They were in just as much trouble as she suspected they were.

She squeezed her eyes shut and hoped that somehow, someway, her dad and the skipper would save them all.

# 12

Dripping wet and out of breath, Marco leaned against the closed hatch. How could John go back out there? The wind, the rain, the weather conditions in general . . . Marco had been so glad to get back inside, even though, with the careening motion of the boat, he wasn't sure how safe being inside actually was.

And what was that crash they heard?

He swung his flashlight back down into the cabin. His mom's face was pale, and her eyes were shut as her lips moved silently, praying, he supposed. She had an arm tightly around Nacho's shoulder, his face hidden, buried in her chest, while Sarah sank down to the floor at the bottom of the stairs and cried.

Marco felt a little like crying himself. He was

scared, more afraid than he'd ever been. The unknown: that was the thing that made his heart pound; the unpredictable nature of . . . well . . . nature.

And the helplessness. That frightened him too. No matter how skilled or experienced or talented Captain Norm was at sailing, it was possible the storm would win; take the boat down. And with it, all of them.

He needed to help.

Marco shoved his shoulder into the hatch, braced his legs, and pushed.

"Marco!" his mom yelled. "What are you doing?"

He didn't answer. Instead he focused on the door and managed to crack it open enough to jam his foot in the door. He shoved his way through, and the wind slammed the hatch behind him.

Rain and seawater pelted him in the face, forcing him to squint against the deluge. Suddenly, hands gripped him. John's face was in his. "What are you doing?" he shouted. "You need to go back down!"

With the back of his free hand, Marco swiped the water out of his eyes and peered behind John. The cracked mast had fallen sideways and lay across the deck. Ahab was there by the mast, perched over something.

Something? Or . . .

Marco couldn't breathe and his eyes widened.

Ahab was licking his master's face. Captain Norm lay on the deck, motionless.

Marco's mouth fell open.

John grabbed him by the shoulders. The storm was so loud he had to shout into Marco's face to even be heard. "Norm is gone! I have to try and call for help."

"Didn't he already do that?" yelled Marco, choking on the water that blasted into his mouth whenever he opened it.

John didn't answer. He grabbed on to the fallen mast for balance and made his way over to Ahab. He took hold of the dog's collar and dragged him back to Marco. "Get him below!"

Marco gripped him, but Ahab was determined to go back to Norm. The deck was glutted with water, and Marco's feet slipped out from under him, but he held on to the dog's collar. Ahab tried to drag him back over to the skipper, but John got behind the dog and pushed. Marco got to his knees, and they managed to pull open the door and get the dog inside before the hatch blew shut again. Marco stood outside, a fierce roaring in his ears as the storm beat at him.

"Marco!" yelled John.

Marco faced his stepdad.

John said, "Don't tell them! About the skipper. Not yet! Okay?"

Marco nodded. They pulled the hatch open and Marco slipped inside. Sarah knelt beside Ahab, wiping him with a kitchen towel. His mom grabbed Marco's arm, her eyes darting all over his face. "Are you okay?"

He had barely nodded when she added, "Don't do that again!"

Nacho told him, "I thought you weren't coming back!"

Marco set a hand on Nacho's head. "Sorry. Can't get rid of me that easy."

A few minutes later, the hatch slammed and Marco jumped as Nacho cried out and both his mom and Sarah shrieked.

John nearly fell back down the stairs, soaked to the bone, his eyes wide. "He's gone."

"Who?" asked Sarah.

John was panting, and had to stop and breathe before speaking again. "The skipper. Norm." He shook his head, and droplets of water flew from his hair. "He's gone."

Marco was confused.

John had told him to wait, and now he was telling them? Before he could open his mouth, his stepfather looked at him. "I mean he is *gone*, as in not on the boat anymore."

Marco felt his stomach drop and Sarah gasped.

Nacho looked up, his eyes red from crying. "Where? Where did he go?!"

Sarah cried, "He can't just leave us!"

"He wouldn't just leave us, sweetheart," said John.

"Are you sure?" Yvonna asked. "How can he be gone?"

"I'm not sure." John slumped down on the floor. "I went to use the distress call, but I couldn't get it to work, and then . . . he was gone." He put a hand to his forehead.

Yvonna said, "We need to look for him! He could be hurt—"

Marco said, "It's terrible out there."

As if to emphasize his point, the boat tilted horrendously to one side and paused there, causing Marco's heart to stop, before the craft finally righted itself, only to tilt to the other side.

"Dad, what do we do?" Sarah's voice was small and shaky, and John held out his arms to her. She crawled over to him, Ahab at her heels, and he embraced her as he looked at the others.

John cleared his throat. "We're not going to go looking for the captain."

Yvonna started to say something, but John's expression made her stop. He said, "He was . . . he was already gone when we went up there. I mean—"

"Dead?" asked Nacho. His voice was shaky.

Marco put a hand on his shoulder. "Yeah. We think it was the mast."

His mom's forehead wrinkled. "The mast? What's wrong with the mast?"

Marco exchanged a glance with his stepfather, who nodded and said, "The sound we heard was the mast falling. It's broken."

As Nacho ran to their mom, Sarah shoved her face into Ahab's fur.

Marco remembered the headset. "We can call for help!" He shined the flashlight at the electronics panel he'd found earlier.

John made his way over and sat down in the chair. He put on the headset and starting pushing buttons. "SOS! SOS!" He paused. "Hello! SOS! SOS!" He kept flipping switches, shouting, "SOS!" now and then. After a few minutes, he took off the headset and put it on the table. He shook his head. "I don't think it worked."

Sarah asked, "What do we do?"

“We have to ride it out,” John said. “That’s all we can do.” He swallowed. “We have no choice.”

Marco made his way over to his mom, who put her other arm around his shoulder and squeezed. Marco had questions.

He wanted to ask, *What if the boat starts leaking?*

*What if the boat capsizes?*

*What if—*

But then he realized he already knew the answer.

Worst case?

They would go down with the boat.

Best case?

They would all be adrift in the ocean during a storm.

Either way, the chances of surviving . . .

Marco leaned his head on his mother, scrunched his eyes shut, and pretended she had never met John; they were still back in Texas, and had never even left home.

# 13

All night long they huddled in the cabin as the furious sea tossed *Moonflight* about, sometimes so violently that Sarah held her breath, thinking they were done for. She couldn't sleep, not with her heart pounding and the rest of her body a trembling knot as she braced herself for each dip and sway of the boat. At least she was over her seasickness.

Yvonna, however, had crawled into the small bathroom earlier and was vomiting for a while. Sarah knew how she felt and couldn't help but muster a little sympathy for her.

Ahab stayed by Sarah. He whined now and then, but he made no move to try to escape the boat, which seemed to help calm Sarah. The dog seemed to know things, and if he was content to stay on board the boat, then maybe . . . well, she hoped anyway, that it meant they would be okay.

Finally, she gave up and laid her head down in her dad's lap. She knew she'd never fall asleep, so she squeezed her eyes shut and tried to pretend she was in her room back in California. She lay there for hours, hoping they'd make it out alive.

And then she woke up on her side by herself, and there was . . . nothing.

Well, not nothing in the sense of absolute silence, but nothing in the sense of no rushing, howling wind, or beating rain and waves. There was no movement. She heard a trickle of water that seemed to come and go.

Was it over?

She sat up in the dim cabin, lit only by the lantern, whose battery-powered glow was fading by the minute. Her dad leaned back against the wall, his mouth hanging open as he quietly snored, Yvonna's head on his lap. The boys were on their sides on the floor, both of them still asleep.

Sarah stood, but couldn't stay upright. The boat was tilted to one side.

And the boat was still. Not moving.

She quickly undid the straps of her smelly life jacket and tossed it as far away as she could. "Ugh."

And then she realized what was missing. *Who* was missing.

"Ahab?" Her voice was a whisper, but should have been loud enough for the dog to hear if he was on board the boat. She walked through the galley and over to the stairs. She looked up at daylight through the open hatch, then began to climb.

She'd been wrong. The hatch wasn't simply open, it was gone entirely, ripped off the hinges by the fury of the storm. Sarah stepped on deck and was immediately warmed by the sun. The sky was blue, not a cloud to be seen. She froze.

The main mast was gone. All that remained was the bottom third, shards of wood where the rest of it had been broken off.

The deck was clear; everything that had been there the last time she'd been on top was gone, swept overboard. "Ahab?"

She stepped to the side of the boat that was tipped up, grabbed on to the side rail, and looked over. She gasped.

Only a few hundred yards away lay an *island.*

*Moonflight* had come to rest in a picturesque turquoise cove with a pristine white sand beach and thick, luscious palm trees. Her gaze went upward. Far beyond the initial line of trees, a green-topped mountain rose high above the rest. The place looked like a painting, far too beautiful to be real.

Sarah gulped. Had they made it? Was this where they had been heading all along?

She heard a bark. "Ahab?"

The dog appeared between two palm trees and ran down onto the beach. As gentle waves lapped at his paws, he sat there, barking at Sarah. Then whining. Then barking again.

"What is he doing?"

The sailboat shuddered, and Sarah looked down.

They had sideswiped a rock, which had impaled the hull, rendering the boat immobile. But Sarah saw water seeping in and out of the edges of the hole. Was Ahab trying to tell her that they needed to get off? He had been right about the storm, that was for sure.

Sarah stuck her head through the doorway and yelled, "Get up!" *Moonflight* shuddered again. "Now!" she screamed.

Her dad's face appeared at the bottom of the stairs. "We've stopped?"

Sarah nodded. "There's an island. But we ran into a rock and I think the boat is going to sink."

John came up beside her and froze when he saw the island. "It's so beautiful."

"Dad!" Sarah grabbed his arm. "The boat!"

John appraised the situation. "The keel must be touching the bottom, or some other rocks. That's why we're leaning. We seem to be pretty solid, but that could change with the tide. We probably shouldn't waste time in getting off." He disappeared and Sarah heard him calling to the others. Then he called up to her. "We need to grab all the supplies we can. Is the dinghy still there?"

"No! Yes! I don't know!" She threw her hands in the air. "What's a dinghy?"

Her dad took a deep breath, like he needed extra patience or something. "It's a small boat. Like a lifeboat. It was on the stern—the back—of the boat."

Sarah made her way to the stern and looked over. A small white boat, which looked barely big enough for a couple of people, was attached by a rope. "Yeah!" she yelled. "I see it." She didn't add any details, like the fact that the dinghy was upside down in the water; her dad could find out that bad news on his own.

John joined her on deck, and set down a basket full

of cans and boxes. He looked over the side and sighed. "I'm going down there. I hope it still floats."

He handed his glasses to Sarah, then put his legs over the side and jumped into the water with a splash. Sarah watched as her dad was able to right the dinghy and climb into it. He grinned up at her. "Lucky for us, someone did a great job lashing these oars to it. Seems to be fine! Just a little wet. Can you pass down that basket? Put my glasses in it, would you?"

Sarah set the glasses gently on top, then tried to lift the basket, but it was too heavy. She dragged it over to the side. "What do I do now?"

She heard a thump and whirled around. Marco had just dropped a loaded mesh bag onto the deck. He gazed at the island. "Whoa. Sweet." He peered over the side at John. "How are we gonna lower this stuff?"

John asked, "Do you see a rope of any kind?"

Marco lifted up the lid of one of the benches. "Yeah." He pulled out a frayed, knotted-up line. "I guess this qualifies. Hold on." He slipped off his life jacket. "This thing is too hot." He slid the line through the basket handles, and dropped it over the side, lowering it slowly to John, who caught it and undid the line. "Perfect. Send down some more."

As Marco started to do the same to the mesh bag, he looked over at Sarah. "Are you just standing there? There's a lot more stuff down there to unload." He scowled. "Unless you're too busy doing *nothing*."

Sarah stuck out her tongue at him, whirled on one toe, and headed over to the stairs. Down in the cabin, she found Yvonna and Nacho had taken off their life jackets and were furiously grabbing food and water. But she focused on the corner, and their pile of suitcases. Sarah grabbed hers and dragged it up the stairs. She wheeled it over to Marco. He glanced at her, took ahold of it, and called, "Heads up!" Then he dropped it.

Sarah leapt over to the side and looked down.

Her suitcase had landed outside the dinghy, but her dad had snagged a corner of it and was hauling it in.

Sarah shoved Marco. "You did that on purpose!"

He shrugged. "Maybe there are more important things than your stupid clothes."

Sarah glared at him and went back downstairs.

# 14

After the third load up the stairs, Marco stopped counting. His mom and Nacho and Sarah had put food and supplies in whatever kind of carrier they could find, even pillowcases, and he just kept hauling things over the railing and lowering them to the dinghy. John had made one trip to the beach in the dinghy so far, and was about to leave for the second. Marco called down, "I think we only have one more load."

John said, "And that'll be everything?"

Marco nodded. "Pretty much the food and water supplies."

John sat down for a moment. His hair was plastered to his scalp with sweat and his face was red; maybe from the exertion, maybe from the sun. Marco couldn't tell. John said, "What about other stuff? We're going to have to make a camp until we get rescued. I mean, that could be later today or maybe not until tomorrow. So if we have to spend the night, we will want blankets. And matches for a fire."

Marco nodded. "I'm on it." He appreciated that John was treating him like an equal in the endeavor, not talking down to him. He also liked that he and John seemed to be running the show, because the others did whatever Marco asked them to do, no questions. Marco went over to the top of the stairs and called down, "Bring some blankets. And matches or a lighter!"

Nacho's head popped into view. "I found a box of matches!" He held it up, his hands shiny.

"Nice," said Marco. He wondered how much hand sanitizer would be required to get his brother through the morning. He held up a hand. "Toss them here, I'll keep them dry."

Nacho took a step but tripped as he began his throw. The box of matches hit the rope railing and came to rest on the very edge of the deck.

Marco dove for them, his fingertips grasping air just as the box slid over the side. "Are you kidding me?"

Marco watched the box slowly dampen and sink. He blew out a breath. "Great."

Nacho got to his feet. "Sorry."

Marco shot him a look and went back to what he was doing.

Their mom climbed up the stairs and set a plastic tub at Marco's feet. She was sweaty, and stopped to push her hair out of her face as she gazed out at the lagoon. "Oh, this place is so lovely!"

"What's in here?" asked Marco.

Yvonna said, "I've got some dishes and silverware in here. I suppose we'll have a few meals here before we get rescued, we might as well be civilized about it." She shoved a hand over her mouth and ran to the side of the boat, then leaned over and threw up.

"Mom? You okay?"

She nodded.

Marco found a bottle of water in the pile and handed it to her. "You feel better?"

Yvonna nodded, then took a sip, rinsed out her mouth, and spit. She took a few swallows as she wiped some sweat off her face with the back of her hand. "I think maybe I ate something that didn't agree with me. Or maybe it's still the motion sickness. I'm sure I'll feel better once I'm on dry land." She added, "So let's not mention it to John, okay? He's got enough on his mind."

"Sure." Marco went back over to the stern and watched as John reached the beach. Ahab greeted him, tail wagging, and stayed there as he unloaded.

Just then, the sailboat shifted under Marco's feet, sliding to an even steeper tilt.

He heard a scream from below. His mom yelled down into the hold, "Nacho! Sarah! Get up here! We need to get off!"

Nacho and Sarah scrambled up the stairs, breathless. Sarah asked, "Where's my dad?"

Marco pointed to shore, and the boat shifted again. Sarah yelled to shore, "Dad! The boat is moving!"

John looked up, startled, and shoved the dinghy into the water. He rowed furiously toward them, as they all filled their arms with the last of the things piled on the deck. When he reached the boat, they passed the last of it down to him. "Okay, everybody down here."

Yvonna asked, "Will we all fit?"

John said, "Yeah, let's go."

Yvonna looked at Nacho. "Where's your life jacket?"

"It was too hot." Nacho pointed out, "You took yours off too."

"I know," said his mom. "There's no time. Come on, you go first." His mom took one of his arms and Marco held on to the other, and they lowered him over the side until John could get ahold of his legs, then take him the rest of the way. "Sarah next."

They did the same to Sarah, and as she dropped into the dinghy, it swayed, almost tipping over. John said, "We need to dump stuff over. We can't take everyone."

"We might need that stuff!" yelled Marco. "Just take them. Mom and I will wait here."

Yvonna glanced at him and nodded. She told John, "He's right. Just go, take them, and come back for us."

John opened his mouth to argue, but Marco said, "Go. We're wasting time arguing." John nodded and said nothing more as he began to row back to the beach. With wide eyes, Sarah and Nacho huddled in the bottom of the overloaded dinghy as it rocked from side to side, threatening to capsize.

Yvonna set a hand on Marco's arm. "I'm proud of you. John couldn't have done this without you."

Marco didn't say anything as he watched the dinghy slowly make it to shore. As soon as Sarah stepped out of the boat, Ahab was all over her. Nacho hopped out and John quickly unloaded the dinghy and pushed off, rowing back toward HMS *Moonflight.*

"You ready, Mom? I can try to lower you down—" The sailboat jerked under them, so hard that Marco stumbled and almost fell. His mom grabbed the side and hung on as the boat tipped so much that Marco lost his balance and started to slide down the deck. "Mom!"

Yvonna grabbed his arm with one hand as she clutched the side of the boat with the other. The boat continued to tilt until they were nearly vertical, hanging from the side. "Marco, climb up me if you can!"

Marco looked down at his feet, and the twenty-or-so-foot drop to the sea. He reached up with his arm and grabbed ahold of his mom's shoulder, trying to get a grip to pull himself up. "Don't let go!" When he had both of his hands on her shoulders, hanging there, he said, "Grab the boat with both your hands!"

"I'm not letting go of you!" But as she started to get a better grip with her hand, she slipped, and they both fell, plummeting all the way down the slanted deck, right into the water, without any life jackets on. Marco took a breath right before they plunged in, then kicked his feet and bobbed right back up. "Mom!" he gasped.

Yvonna popped up right beside him, gasping, her wet, dark hair plastered to her face. She reached out. "You okay?"

"I'm here!" John was right beside them with the dinghy, and held out a hand to Marco. He shook his head. "Take my mom first." John didn't even argue as he nodded at Marco, first helping his wife into the boat, then reaching out his hand for Marco.

When they were safe inside, John rowed them back to the beach.

# 15

Sarah sat on the beach in the hot sun, looking out into the blue waves. The others were sitting a little ways away from her. She still felt like she was swaying, so she shut her eyes. That only made the feeling worse, so she opened them again. Still, she was so relieved to be off the boat and on dry, unmoving land—especially such beautiful dry, unmoving land—that she let Ahab lick her face as long as he wanted. He probably deserved it, after warning them to get off the boat. She held his head still for a moment. "You knew, didn't you, boy? You knew it was dangerous."

Out in the cove, *Moonflight* hadn't slipped any farther, and actually seemed to have tipped back until it was nearly level, perched halfway out of the water as the hull stayed hung up on the rock. John came and stood there, looking out at the water as he caught his breath. He reached down and ruffled her hair.

She asked, "Is someone coming to get us?"

Her dad said, "The captain filed a float plan." Then he slapped a hand to his forehead.

"What's wrong?" asked Sarah.

"He said we'd spend three days on the island, and then he probably allowed a day to return." He sighed. "So unless the skipper was able to get out a distress call, I suspect no one will start looking until those days are up."

"So we might be here for days before they come looking for us?" Sarah felt tears well up. "Is this even the island we were heading to?"

"I don't know for sure, sweetie." He put his arm around her. "We have supplies. And it sure is a lovely place to be marooned, I'll give it that."

He shaded his eyes and turned slowly around in a circle, stopping to face the first row of trees. He pointed and called out to Yvonna. "See those trees?"

Sarah looked where he was pointing.

Three very tall trees had grown together, their thick, wide limbs sprouting out of the enormous trunks. The numerous branches—laden with green leaves and pink flowers—formed a huge umbrella-like canopy that shaded a massive stretch of grassy ground.

"I read my *Flora and Fauna of the South Pacific* on the plane," said Nacho. "Those are monkey pod trees! They're called that because those flowers grow seed pods that you can actually eat."

John said, "Well, I think those *monkey pod trees* would make a good shelter. Let's make camp under them."

Sarah reluctantly pushed Ahab away and stood up, almost losing her balance as she still felt like she was on a boat. She hoped that feeling would go away, but she grabbed ahold of Ahab for help. He stayed right at her side, wagging his tail, his tongue hanging out as he panted. With Ahab at her heels, she dragged her suitcase through the sand, stopping every few feet to catch her breath. "Stupid wheels." Finally, she reached the shady grass under the trees and let her suitcase fall on its side.

Marco dropped a plastic bin right next to it. "There's more stuff to carry."

"I'm catching my breath," snapped Sarah.

Nacho dumped a load right next to the other stuff and smiled up at her. "Our own desert island! Isn't it cool?"

"Yeah." Sarah scowled. "Just *fabulous*."

Nacho patted the tree trunk nearest him. "Did you know that these trees are also called rain trees?"

"No, I did not know that." Sarah rolled her eyes.

Nacho nodded. "See how the grass under the trees is really green?"

Sarah glanced down at her feet, where the grass did seem extraordinarily green and lush. "Yeah."

"First, there's the canopy." Nacho pointed overhead to the branches that formed an umbrella over them. "That keeps it shady and cool under here. Then at night, the leaves curl up, so rain gets past to the ground easier. And the reason the grass is super green is from the nitrogen, which comes from the seed pods."

Sarah sighed. "Good to know."

After being stuck with the Murillo family in such tight quarters all night, she was not about to stand around getting a lecture about the life of trees from a far too chatty ten-year-old. She headed back over to the pile and grabbed two jugs of water. Ahab sniffed at one as she walked, then, with his long, pink tongue, he licked the outside.

"Are you thirsty?" When she reached the other things, she set the jugs down and dug in the plastic bin until she found a bowl. She poured in some water and set it on the grass. Ahab lapped at the bowl, draining it in seconds. He looked up at Sarah, swishing his tail so hard his bottom swayed from side to side.

"More?" she asked. Without waiting for an answer, she filled the bowl again.

Marco said, "Hey. Don't waste all the water on a dog."

Sarah put her hands on her hips. "He has to drink too."

Her dad reached them with an armload of supplies. "What's going on?"

Marco said, "She's giving all our drinking water to the dog."

John looked at her and scratched his chin. "How much drinking water do we have?"

Yvonna came over then, and pointed to the jugs. "Those two, and then a couple of cases of bottled water."

"So not a lot," said John. He circled around and looked into the trees. "It looks like a pretty big island. There could definitely be some fresh water somewhere." He wiped his hands together. "First I'd better make a fire. Did I see a bag with emergency supplies?"

Yvonna pulled a red canvas bag out of the pile and handed it to him. He reached in and pulled out the flint. "I'm not entirely sure how to do this, but I do have a degree in engineering. It can't be that hard."

Marco said, "Wow, too bad we don't have any matches." He glared at Nacho.

Nacho ignored him and said, "I can help! I've been studying for my Eco-Scout camping badge."

Marco mumbled, "Your hands might get dirty."

Nacho scowled. "At least *I* know how to do it, Marco! Do you?"

Marco shrugged. "Fine. Go for it."

John hesitated for a moment, but then handed the flint to Nacho. "Tell me what you need."

Nacho stared at the flint. "Um . . . first we need rocks." Sarah and John helped find rocks. Nacho said, "We need to arrange them in a circle." He pointed to a spot about ten feet away from their makeshift camp under the trees. Marco and John got the rocks and set them up. Nacho said, "Now we need some tinder. Like some small sticks?"

They went off searching, and Sarah came back with a bunch of small sticks, which she set in the center of the rocks. A few minutes later, her dad brought husk from a coconut.

"Where'd you find the coconut?" asked Marco.

"It's just the husk," said John. "Someone must have opened it up."

Sarah frowned. "Who would have opened it up?"

Marco said, "Maybe the last people who were shipwrecked here?"

Sarah glared at him, then focused her attention back to Nacho. "What do we do now?"

"You need to . . ." He trailed off. He bit his lip and reached out. He pinched small pieces of the husk between two fingers and gingerly piled them on top of the small stack of kindling. "Is there a knife?"

John knelt down beside him, holding up a long blade.

Nacho handed him the flint. "Okay, now you need to take—"

"Nacho," said Marco. "Why don't you just do it?" He didn't think his brother would, but he was tired of it taking so long.

"Okay." But Nacho just stood there, not saying anything. "I'll be right back." He ran over to a jug of water and poured some into his hands, rubbed them together, and wiped them on his shorts. He looked up to see everyone watching him. "I wanted to wash off the hand sanitizer."

"That's a first," mumbled Marco.

"It could be flammable," said Nacho. He grabbed a thick bunch of the coconut husk, cradling the scratchy fluff in his hand. He took a deep breath and blew it out. "Okay. Just strike the blade on the flint, like really quick, so the spark will go onto the husk."

"Careful!" called Yvonna.

John carefully struck the flint and a spark fell into the husk. Nothing happened.

Nacho said, "I wasn't ready. Try it again."

"Seriously?" said Marco. "I don't think you know what you're doing."

Nacho ignored him. He took a wider stance, squared his shoulders, and told his stepfather, "Try again. I'm ready."

Once again, John struck the flint and a spark hopped into the husk. Nacho immediately held the husk up to his face and blew gently.

Bits of the husk glowed red and a wisp of smoke drifted up.

Nacho blew again, and a flame burst up. He quickly crouched down and set the husk on top of the kindling, then added more husk and small sticks, feeding the flame until it was snapping.

"You did it." Marco sounded surprised. "Way to go."

Nacho grinned and looked up at his brother.

John said, "Good job!" and Yvonna clapped.

Sarah sat down beside the fire, watching the flames grow as Nacho gradually added more and more wood to the flame. Finally, she said, "That's a great fire, Nacho."

He looked up at her. "Thanks. I've been studying and I knew what to do." He lifted and lowered a shoulder. "I just wasn't sure that I could do it." He looked very pleased with himself.

John said, "Since we have a fire master here, it might be time to do some exploring." He looked toward the trees.

"You're not thinking of going in there, are you?" asked Yvonna. She frowned. "It might not be safe."

He shrugged. "Better to find water before we really need it."

Yvonna said, "I don't think you should go off on your own."

Ahab sat next to Sarah and she put her face in his neck. She didn't want to have to worry about water or how long they would have to be there. She just wanted to be at home. Instead, there she was, on a stupid island, listening as her dad and stepmother argued about him going into the trees alone.

"Okay," John said. "You're right. I won't go alone."

Yvonna said, "Thank you."

"Ready to go?" John asked.

Sarah nodded and stood up, then froze. Her dad's eyes were trained on Marco. He wasn't even talking to her. She watched as her dad and Marco disappeared into the trees.

Yvonna asked Sarah, "Why don't you help me set up camp?"

Sarah shook her head. "I'm going down to the beach."

"I really think you should stay here." Yvonna frowned.

Nacho said, "Yeah, you can help me arrange the medical and cleaning supplies."

"No, thanks." Sarah grabbed Ahab's collar and walked down toward the water.

Yvonna called after her, "Stay where I can see you!"

Sarah rolled her eyes. She wasn't about to let her stepmother tell her what to do. "Come on, boy." But Ahab seemed more than content to go wherever she did. She let go and he stayed right by her side, wagging his wet, sandy tail. She sighed. "You are totally going to need a bath, aren't you?"

As if he heard her, he charged right into the waves, let them pummel him a bit, then ran back out. "No!"

Sarah held up her hands just as Ahab started to shake his fur, drenching her with seawater.

"Ugh." She wiped off her face with the bottom of her shirt, then gave Ahab a stern look.

He simply wagged his tail, staring at her with an open mouth as he panted.

"Maybe we should go exploring too, huh, boy?" Sarah glanced back up at the beach at Yvonna and Nacho, who were busy setting up camp under the monkey pod trees. "They won't miss us." She started to walk away from the area, toward the edge of the trees. Ahab didn't follow.

Sarah stopped and waited for him. "Come on." She slapped her hand on her leg a few times. "Let's go."

Ahab took one long look back at Yvonna and Nacho and whined a little bit before trotting over to Sarah. She headed around the curve of beach, and soon she was out of sight of the camp.

Just being alone made her feel a little better. She felt like she'd gone for days without one shred of privacy, and she was amazed at how simply getting out of sight of everyone else made her relax. Ahab stayed at her heels as she walked along the beach, which seemed to stretch for close to a mile, always lined with palm trees.

"This place is bigger than I thought," Sarah said.

She picked up a piece of driftwood and threw it out into the water. Ahab stayed by her side. "Not much of a fetcher, huh?" She sat down on the sand and Ahab plopped beside her, his snout on his paws. "I'm sorry about your master." Ahab didn't move, but his eyes turned up to gaze at her. "Maybe I'm your new master, huh?" Ahab lifted his head and panted, his long pink tongue lolling about.

Sarah smiled. "I'll take care of you, boy. I promise." She stroked his head. "You'll like California." She sighed. Unfortunately, California, and home, felt a world away.

Suddenly, Ahab did an about-face, staring at the line of trees about ten yards from where they stood. He growled.

Sarah froze. "What?"

Vines filled the dark space between the trees, and she couldn't see anything. Then, there was a rustling. She quickly knelt by Ahab and hugged his neck, her heart pounding. The dog growled again, his throat vibrating against her skin, but he made no move to run.

With a rush, a kangaroo bounded out onto the beach, paused to look at them, then bounced off down the beach, vanishing as quickly as it had appeared.

Ahab whined as Sarah felt her mouth drop open.

She looked up at the hot sun and wiped some sweat off her forehead. She needed some water. And some food. Most definitely a nap. The sun was obviously making her see things that weren't there.

Because she'd seen marsupials before, many times.

But never one with claws the size of a lion's.

Sarah was eye level with Ahab. "Let's keep this to ourselves, okay, boy?"

Ahab looked at her with puzzled eyes, then, with one large swath of tongue, licked her face in agreement.

# 16

Marco was content to follow John through the trees. Roots and vines curled everywhere, making the footing rather tricky. The undergrowth was thicker in some places than others, so he found himself having to walk with his eyes on the ground. They had walked about half a mile when Marco ran right into John's back, not realizing he had stopped. "*Ooomph.*"

"Sorry," said John. "It's just . . ."

Marco looked up. "What is it?"

John was staring ahead. "What does that look like to you?" His gaze was trained up high, above the treetops. What had looked like a simple green mountain from the beach had taken on a different shape now that they were closer.

Marco gulped. "Is that a volcano?"

"That was my first thought," said John. "It's probably extinct, otherwise it wouldn't be so green." He smiled at Marco. "Nothing to worry about." He shrugged. "It's not every day you see a volcano."

Marco nodded. "I guess not."

John started walking again.

Marco continued following, but this time he stole glances up at the volcano now and then. The green peak seemed quite far away from where they were, which made him wonder exactly how big the island was. Marco's heart pounded a little faster, and not just from the walking. If the island had a volcano that seemed so far away, then there was a huge part of the island left to explore. There could be anything on the island: hopefully water, maybe food of some sort, but there could also be other things that weren't so pleasant. Other—possibly dangerous—things.

They came to a clearing, edged by trees whose vines dripped down to the ground. John pointed to the far end of the clearing, which was bordered by a hillside. "Look at that."

"A cave?" asked Marco.

"I think so," said John. He looked around, and then headed over there, Marco close on his heels. John stepped inside and immediately came back out. "Too dark. I didn't even think to bring a flashlight."

Marco let out the breath that he didn't even know he'd been holding. Although he wouldn't refer to himself as claustrophobic, he was not exactly a fan of enclosed spaces, so he was hardly disappointed that they wouldn't be exploring the cave.

John pointed. "Well, look at that."

Nearly hidden under an especially thick section of vines was a wooden structure. "Is that a . . . *house*?" Marco asked. Who would live on a deserted island? "Let's go see!" He headed that way.

"Hold on now!" John followed close behind.

The structure wasn't especially large, maybe fifteen feet wide by twenty feet long, and the wooden roof came to a peak not more than ten feet in the air. But to Marco, it certainly looked like a house.

A small porch popped off the front of it, and Marco put a foot on the boards, testing them before he put his full weight on.

John said, "Careful." He put a foot on the porch himself. "Seems sturdy."

Marco stepped closer up and bounced a few times. "Coming?"

"Better let me go first." John covered the few feet to the front door and knocked.

"You think someone lives here?" Marco looked around. The place seemed rather run-down, with moss on the roof and a bird's nest in one corner of the porch roof.

John shook his head. "Just being polite." There was no knob on the door, so he pulled on a string sticking out of a hole, and pushed the door open, then stepped inside.

Marco pushed his way in behind until he was standing on the solid wooden floor. A roughly hewn wooden table with two chairs lay to his right. Two wooden plates, two glasses, and silverware sat at each place, dried bread and moldy meat on each plate.

Marco wrinkled his nose. "Looks like someone got interrupted during dinner."

"I think we should leave," said John. But then he looked down, and stared at his feet. Their footsteps had left marks in the layer of dust.

"What?" asked Marco.

His stepfather scratched his head. "This floor. It's . . . oak."

"So?" Marco wondered what that had to do with anything.

"Oak isn't tropical." John shook his head. "It wouldn't grow here. So someone . . . whoever built this place . . . brought this wood from somewhere else."

That didn't matter much to Marco, who stepped over to the window and pulled aside a ratty curtain. While the trees outside shaded the place, a bit of extra light came in so they could see the small room. A ramshackle wooden structure, about seven feet long, took up the better part of the far wall.

Marco asked, "Is that a bed?"

John scratched his head. "It kinda looks like it, but it's far too long. Unless an NBA player used to live here."

Marco checked out the rest of the room.

The back wall had a rustic fireplace made from rough black stone, and ashes still lay inside. John knelt and touched them with his hand. He looked a bit sheepish as he shrugged. "I was only checking. Ice cold."

Just as Marco stepped closer to the fireplace, a rush of wings flew out of the opening and he yelled, startled.

John fell backward on the floor and his glasses fell off.

Marco froze as he got a glimpse of the bird that flew past him on its way out the door. He asked, "Did you see that?"

John found his glasses and put them back on. "What? Was it a bird?"

Marco was silent for a moment. Then he nodded, because to say what he was thinking—*That didn't look like any bird I've ever seen*—would have sounded dumb. He still felt like he was in motion from the boat; maybe that was going to his head, affecting his vision maybe. After all, no bird has . . .

He shook his head, pushing away the thought, because it simply could not have been real.

"What kind?" John asked.

Marco's heart pounded. He said, "I have no idea."

John smiled. "Maybe it's in that bird book of yours."

Marco looked out the door the way the bird had flown. "Yeah. Maybe." But something told him that he wouldn't find that bird in that book. Or in any book for that matter. His hands had begun to tremble. He wanted to leave that place.

John got to his feet, then pulled out a chair and sat down. "Solid. Someone knew what they were doing."

Marco asked, "Do you think whoever lived here . . . still lives here?"

"No," said John, maybe too quickly. His eyes moved slowly over the table, the place settings, then lingered on the abandoned meal.

"Maybe there was a storm," said Marco. "And the people had to leave right away?"

"Maybe," said John. "Or . . . maybe the people here were waiting for a boat, like we are, and it came during dinner. Whatever happened, no one has been here for a long time." He tilted his head to the fireplace. "That obviously hasn't been used recently. I mean, if birds are nesting in it . . ." He stood up. "I'm going to look around outside. You coming?"

Marco nodded and began to follow John out the door. But then he stopped. Something glittered under the bed. He walked over and squatted beside it. Whatever it was lay a few inches under, so he reached in and his hand closed around something small and cool and smooth. He pulled it out and opened his hand.

On his palm lay a glass bottle of some sort, with a pyramid-shaped stopper and strange gold legs. Something inside the bottle—perfume?—swirled. He pulled out the stopper, held up the bottle to his nose, and sniffed. A lovely scent, like some exotic flower he'd never smelled before, invaded his senses.

As did a woman's voice: *Come back.*

"Mom?" Marco looked at the door.

No one was there.

"John!" he yelled.

A distant "Yeah! Over here!" came from outside.

Marco's heart began to pound. He knew he had heard something. He shoved the stopper back in and rolled the bottle over in his hand, looking for a mark of the maker, a name. All his mom's perfumes had names on them. But there was nothing.

The outside of the bottle was completely blank.

Once more he held the bottle up, removed the stopper, and sniffed.

Again, that heavenly scent. And, again, the woman's voice. *Please come back.*

Suddenly, the walls pressed in on him. His chest felt heavy and he couldn't breathe. Marco shoved the bottle into the pocket of his board shorts and ran outside. He stooped over, hands on his knees, sucking in air until his head felt clear.

Marco stood back up.

He had to be imagining things. First, that . . . *bird.* Then the woman's voice. Maybe the sun and the heat . . . maybe he needed to drink some water. With a quick glance back at the house, he headed over to John, who stood under a tree.

John cradled something in his palms as he glanced up at Marco. He frowned. "You look like you saw a ghost. What's wrong?"

Marco caught his breath and shook his head. "Nothing. Just . . . I thought you'd left. I didn't want to get lost."

"I wouldn't leave you," said his stepfather, sounding a bit insulted, maybe even hurt, at the idea.

"I know." Trying to change the subject, not wanting to think about what he'd heard—or thought he'd heard—Marco looked down at John's hands. "Wait. Are those . . . are those what I think they are?"

"Yeah." John's hands were full of acorns. Slowly, his eyes traveled from his hand, to the trunk of the tree, then up to the branches, laden with more of them. He looked puzzled. "What in the world is an oak tree doing on a tropical island?"

Despite the heat of the day, Marco felt a chill run up his arms.

John dumped the acorns on the ground and wiped his hands on his shorts. He looked back over at the small house. "Well, at least we know there's an option. I mean, if we find ourselves having to spend more than one night here, we'll have an actual roof over our heads." He smiled at Marco and patted his arm. "I mean, whoever used to live there won't mind, right?"

Marco nodded slightly.

"Better head back, your mother will wonder where

we are." John turned the way they'd come, but Marco paused and looked back at the house. He noticed a wooden barrel by the side of the house, in the shadows of an overgrown tree that kept it nearly hidden. "Hey, what's that?" He pointed.

John headed over and Marco followed. By the time he got there, John was already lifting the lid. He grinned. "Rain barrel." He dipped his cupped hand into the water and then lifted it to his nose. He touched his tongue to the water, then dumped it on the ground.

"Is it bad?" asked Marco.

"Nope." John smiled. "It's fresh, not seawater. We better boil it, just to be safe. We can come back tomorrow with some containers." He frowned. "Is that . . ."

"What?" asked Marco.

"Do you hear that?" asked John.

Marco listened for a moment. He heard running water, but the water in the rain barrel was absolutely still.

John took a few steps behind the house and swept aside a curtain of vines. "Well, would you look at that."

Marco followed John through the opening in the vines and froze. A clear, crystal stream flowed at their feet. Lining it on either side were trees laden with fruit: mango and papaya and guava, so ripe that some were bursting. John squatted beside the stream and cupped some water in his hands. He lifted them to his nose and sniffed. Then he stuck out a tongue and tasted. He shook out his hands and stood back up. "I think this is better water than the rain barrel. We still have to be safe and boil it, but this is amazing."

Marco said, "Should we pick some fruit?"

John nodded. "Definitely." He pointed. "But let's follow the stream a little ways first." He headed past the fruit trees and Marco followed, reaching up to pick one of the mangos. He asked, "Do you have a knife with you?"

John nodded and reached into his pocket, then unfolded a pocketknife and held it out to Marco. He cut off a slice and held it out to John, then cut off another and stuck it in his mouth, scraping the fruit off the skin with his teeth. He chewed and swallowed. "Oh, wow."

John grinned. "That is great mango."

They stood and ate that one and two more. Marco's chin and hands were all sticky. He looked up ahead and grinned. "Avocado!"

John shook out an empty mesh bag that he'd stowed in his pocket and handed it to Marco. "Go for it. I'm gonna see what's up ahead."

Marco picked a few dark green ones off the ground

that would be ready immediately, then chose a few lighter ones that would ripen soon. He jogged to catch up with John. The sound of running water got louder as they neared a corner, and then when they rounded it, Marco stopped and stared.

A waterfall rose nearly thirty feet above them, then ended in a pool that fed into the stream.

"That solves that mystery," said John.

Marco dropped the bag of avocados, kicked off his shoes, pulled off his shirt, and cannonballed into the pool. He went down a ways into the clear, warm water, and then surfaced with a whoop. "It's perfect!" he called. As he treaded water, he dipped his face under, wiping the last of the mango remains off.

John took off his glasses and his shirt, stepped out of his shoes and jumped in. He emerged with a grin. "Wow. That feels wonderful."

They swam around a bit, then John said, "We should bring the others here. They'd love it."

Marco floated on his back in the crystal-clear water, staring up at the cloudless blue sky. If they had to be stuck on an island, at least they'd picked a good one. But as he lay there, relaxing, the whole thing seemed so perfect.

Too perfect?

He had a feeling that he wouldn't want to be there at night.

Marco swam over to the grassy side and got out. John did too, and they dried off as best they could, then headed back the way they'd come.

At the fruit trees, they stopped and picked some of each types of fruit. Then they walked past the house.

As they headed out of the clearing, Marco turned and looked at the house one more time. He knew he would come back to that place to help haul the water and pick fruit and swim in the waterfall pool. But only in the daytime. And, if he could help it, he would never spend a night in that house.

Because, for some reason, he had a feeling that whoever had lived there . . . might just mind after all.

# 17

After the hallucination on the beach, Sarah was only too happy to spend the rest of the afternoon helping Yvonna and Nacho set up the camp in the shade. She had hauled a pile of coconuts from a tree down the beach, and then spent the better part of an hour trying to crack one open with rocks, to no avail.

Then she helped Nacho find driftwood to add to the fire, which was blazing. Sarah sat in the sand next to Nacho, holding a stick out, the skewered hot dog on the end dripping juice onto the flames with a sizzle. She hadn't noticed him put hand sanitizer on at all since he'd started the fire. Probably because he seemed as worried about safety as he was about germs.

Nacho said, "I thought you were a vegetarian."

She lifted and lowered one shoulder. "Too hungry to be a vegetarian."

He sighed. "You just wanted to make my mom feel bad, huh?"

Sarah's mouth fell open. The way he said it, straightforward like that—no trace of accusation—made her feel awful. Because it was the truth. She'd picked up the PETA shirt online, but only because she liked animals, not because she wanted to be a vegetarian. "I was mad, I guess."

Nacho slowly rotated his stick. "Marco was too. He didn't want Mom to get married."

"What about you?" asked Sarah.

He shrugged. "Sometimes she seems lonely. I want her to be happy."

Sarah swallowed. She could say the same thing about her dad. "So you're glad they got married?"

"Kinda." He nodded. "I mean, your house is way cooler than ours. I always wanted more brothers and sisters. But it was hard to leave home. I miss my friends."

She hadn't thought about that. They would have had to leave everything back in Texas just so their mom could marry her dad. At least she got to stay in her own house.

Before she could say anything else, John and Marco

returned. John held the bag aloft. "Look what we found! Fruit!"

Yvonna exclaimed, "I love mangos!" She took the bag from John and said, "I'll cut some of these up."

Marco knelt in the sand on the other side of Nacho. He shoved a stick into a hot dog, then held it over the flame.

Yvonna hugged John. "And did you find any water?"

"Yep." John nodded. "A waterfall and a stream!"

Sarah asked, "Nice enough to swim in?"

Her dad nodded. "Yeah, we did! It was like an oasis. We'll go back with containers when we start running low."

"And to go swimming?" asked Nacho.

"Definitely," said John.

Sarah said, "So if we do have to stay here for a few days, it will be safe, right?"

Her dad nodded. "We have fresh water and fruit, and enough food to last until then." He smiled. "We were already heading to an island, and I can't picture a better one."

As they sat there, Sarah watched the palms fluttering in the warm breeze, then gazed around at the stunning alabaster sand and sparkling turquoise waves. She had to admit that, as much as she didn't want to be there, the island was beautiful.

Nacho asked, "Do you think this place has a name?"

Yvonna said, "We should name it."

"Island of the Blue Waters," suggested Nacho.

"Right," Marco scoffed. "Because no other islands have blue water."

Nacho crossed his arms and narrowed his eyes. "So what do you want to call it?"

Marco said, "What about Island of Eco Boy and his Hand Sanitizer?"

"Marco," said Yvonna.

"What about Shipwreck Island?" asked Sarah.

Yvonna quickly raised her hand. "I vote for Shipwreck Island."

John smiled at her. "Me too."

"Fine," said Nacho.

Sarah glanced at Marco and he shrugged, so she said, "Shipwreck Island, it is."

John asked Yvonna if she wanted help slicing the fruit, and they wandered over to the makeshift kitchen.

Sarah's thoughts drifted, zoning out their conversation. She put her hot dog in a bun and shot a glance over at Marco, waiting for him to comment about her eating meat, like Nacho did, but he didn't say anything. He didn't even seem to notice. Marco was very quiet, too quiet, as he simply stared into the flames, his eyes glazed. His hot dog reddened and began to blister.

Sarah said, "I think it's done."

"Huh?" Marco seemed to wake up. "What?"

Sarah pointed at his hot dog. "Unless you prefer charcoal in your bun."

"Oh." Marco yanked back his stick and flipped it over. "Not too bad."

Sarah handed him the bag of buns.

"Thanks." He proceeded to wrap the bun around the dog and yank it off the stick.

Sarah realized that was the longest he'd gone without saying something mean or sarcastic to her.

Nacho asked his brother, "Did you see anything cool?"

Marco took a bite of his hot dog and chewed. "The waterfall. That was awesome."

"What else?" Sarah lifted and lowered a shoulder. "I mean, there must have been more." For once, Sarah was annoyed that he didn't want to talk.

"There was a waterfall. And fruit trees," he said with his full mouth, not taking his eyes off the fire.

Nacho asked, "So what did you see before the waterfall?"

Marco took an especially big bite of hot dog and chewed, not answering. When he had swallowed, he said, "Nothing else."

John came over to the fire and set down a plate with slices of mango, and some quartered papaya. "I wouldn't say that."

Marco shot a glance at him.

John grinned at her and Nacho. "We found a house."

Sarah's eyes widened. "A real house?" As the words left her mouth, she saw a shadow pass over Marco's face as he suddenly looked uncomfortable, or maybe even in pain. He got to his feet and went over to the pile of things from the boat.

Nacho asked, "Can we go live there?"

John shook his head. "It's a ways in." He motioned toward the lagoon. "We need to stay here, near the beach, so that when the boat comes to rescue us, we can see it."

"Oh." Nacho looked as disappointed as Sarah felt. She didn't like being out in the open on the beach like this, much preferring solid walls between her and the outdoors. Not to mention, she really wanted to see that house.

A breeze blew up from the water, causing the flames to flicker. A chill ran up her neck. Sarah looked out at the horizon, where the sun was beginning to lower. "It's not going to storm is it?"

Her dad sank down into the sand beside her and began to roast his own hot dog. "I don't think so."

"What if it does?" she asked.

John shrugged. "We've got a nice shelter in the trees here. We'll be fine." He put an arm around her. "You okay?"

She nodded. "I just want to go home."

"I know." He squeezed her. "Someone is going to rescue us. Soon."

"Until then?" she asked.

He grinned. "Until then we sit here on this beautiful beach with this lovely fire and our fresh fruit and relax." He looked at Nacho. "Right?"

Nacho was well into his third hot dog and could only nod.

Yvonna came and sat down next to John. He took his arm from around Sarah, switched the stick over, and put his other arm around his new wife.

Sarah jumped up and headed down toward the beach.

Marco sat cross-legged in the sand, well above the lapping waves, holding an open book in his lap.

Sarah hesitated, then went over to him. "Wow, you're actually reading?"

Marco didn't reply. He didn't even look up at her. Instead, he paged through the book, snapping the pages as he searched.

Sarah stepped closer. "Is that the bird book off the boat?"

He nodded, but didn't answer.

"Are you looking for something?"

"Yeah." He sighed, and tossed the book into the sand beside him. "Something I can't find."

Sarah sat down a few feet away and picked up the book. She started paging through it. "What kind of bird did you see?" She thought it might be fun to show him up, find what he couldn't.

"Don't bother. It's not in there." Marco sighed and bent his legs, wrapping his arms around them as he stared out at the water.

Although she'd known him for only a few days, she knew it wasn't in his nature to cave like that, give up so easily. In fact, he sounded so dejected that Sarah closed the book. She asked, "What did it look like?"

He mumbled something.

"What?"

Marco said, "That bird—that *thing.*" He shook his head. "I've never seen anything like it before."

Sarah started to say something, something on the order of "You're not exactly a bird expert, there are probably hundreds of birds you've never seen before . . ." but she didn't. Instead, she thought about what she'd seen earlier, or thought she'd seen. She shivered. "What did it look like?"

"I don't know." Marco threw up his hands. "It was this huge bird and I only saw it for a few seconds. It was this red, this amazing bright red, with—" He trailed off.

"With what?" prodded Sarah.

He shook his head. "You won't believe me."

A visual of that kangaroo creature popped into her head. Sarah hoped she sounded as sincere as she felt. "Try me."

Marco put both his hands on his face and rubbed his eyes for a moment. When he dropped his hands, he said, all in one breath, "That bird . . . just wasn't *right.* It had these weird shiny golden eyes and four wings, two big ones in the front and two smaller ones in the back and—"

*Four wings?* The bird book in Sarah's hands began to tremble. She whispered, "And what?"

He scrunched his eyes shut, like he didn't want to

see himself say whatever was coming next. "It had—" He swallowed. "It didn't have a beak. It had . . . a mouth. A mouth full of teeth. Like seriously sharp teeth. What kind of bird has teeth?"

Sarah didn't answer. And her hands kept trembling.

If Marco had seen what he thought he had . . . that meant there was an excellent chance that she had seen what she thought *she* had . . .

Goose bumps rose on her arms.

Marco said, "You think I'm crazy."

Sarah slowly shook her head as she turned to meet his gaze. "I don't."

"Why not?" He rolled his eyes. "I would."

Sarah looked out to the ocean for a moment and watched the sun start to dip below the horizon. She took a deep breath before telling Marco, "Because I saw something too. Something that wasn't exactly . . . right." Before she could tell him about the kangaroo, a wail rose.

The two scrambled to their feet and ran back to the fire as the sound grew in intensity.

Their parents stood by the fire, Yvonna's arms around Nacho, whose eyes were wide.

"Where's it coming from?" asked John.

No one answered.

The sound, a wordless stream of anguish and grief, seemed to come from everywhere at the same time. Sarah dropped the bird book and smashed her hands over her ears. She shut her eyes, hoping it would help, but the sound vibrated in her chest, making it seem like it came from inside her as well as outside her.

Ahab began to howl.

Beneath their feet, the ground trembled. Sarah screamed and reached out for her dad as Marco ran to Yvonna. The five stood in a huddle as the island shook with the sound of the wail.

And then it was gone.

Ahab barked once, then lay down by the fire, his chin on his stretched-out paws.

Once again, they stood on still and stable ground, nothing to hear but the soft lap of waves on the shore and the snapping of the fire.

John started to walk away.

"Dad!" she called after him. "Where are you going?"

He stopped and reached up, took off his glasses, and cleaned them on the bottom of his shirt. Then he replaced them and pointed at the fire. "I think we'd better build that up before nightfall."

Even though she was not the least bit cold, Sarah shivered.

# 18

Marco lay there, but couldn't fall sleep. His mom and Sarah had used blankets and pillows to make up some halfway comfortable beds around the fire, which John had built up so that it roared. Flames flickered several feet overhead. A large pile of wood lay just outside the circle of stone, so they seemed to be set for the night.

The firelight only stretched a few feet beyond their circle, and Marco tried not to look past where the light licked at the darkness. He had seen—and heard—enough for one day; he didn't care to know what else lay beyond their small zone of comfort.

A few feet away, Ahab was curled up between Nacho and Sarah. Now that Marco realized Ahab was an early-warning system, he liked the dog a lot more.

And really, if the dog felt safe enough to sleep, he should be able to. He punched the pillow under his head and lay back down.

His mom and stepfather had their backs to the fire and talked softly. He'd heard them earlier; their plan was to stay awake all night. A little worrisome, really, if they thought they felt the need to stay awake to watch for . . . whatever might be out *there.*

Marco found it impossible to get the picture of that bird thing out of his head. And he wished he'd had time to hear what Sarah had seen. Maybe she hadn't seen anything and just didn't want to be outdone. But his gut told him different. The tone of her voice had been serious, not snarky like she usually was. He believed her when she said she'd seen something. He didn't know how anything could be freakier than that bird.

As he rolled over, he felt a sharp jab in his leg. He reached into his pocket and pulled out the crystal bottle. The fire reflected in it, and Marco shook it slightly. The liquid inside danced, taking on the colors of the flames. He resisted the urge to smell the bottle, as he had before, and stuffed it into the pouch of his sweatshirt before lying back down. Why hadn't he told Sarah about the bottle? Shown it to her?

Marco didn't have an answer.

He shut his eyes, willing sleep to come. Just as he was dozing off, Ahab growled, then began barking.

Marco's eyes popped open and he sat up.

His mom and John were standing up, watching the dog. Ahab barked at the trees, growing louder as he went on.

Sarah and Nacho sat up on their makeshift beds, eyes wide. "Daddy?" called Sarah. "What is it?"

Yvonna went and sat between Nacho and Sarah. She motioned to Marco, and he joined them, standing behind as they watched the dog. Ahab started to move toward the trees, barking so vigorously that spit flew from his snapping jaws. John was closest to him and began to follow, his flashlight beam leading the way. "Boy, what is it?"

Marco saw John freeze as the dog began to lurch toward the trees, growling and barking.

Then his stepfather whipped around, eyes wide, and sprinted back toward them, waving his arms. "Get up! Get up in the trees!" He motioned to the three trees above them.

Ahab suddenly stopped barking and yelped in pain, the sound of his cries fading as he ran off down the beach.

His heart racing, Marco grabbed Nacho and yanked

him to his feet. "Go!" They ran to the closest trunk and Marco boosted Nacho to the lowest branch, and Nacho began to climb. Marco reached for his mom, but she pushed Sarah toward him. Nacho blocked the way up that tree, so Marco grabbed Sarah under the arms and boosted her up into the next closest tree, waited until she'd gotten up a ways, then he scrambled up after Nacho.

"Faster!" Marco yelled. He pushed on Nacho's butt, and his brother was able to reach a higher branch where he plopped down and told Marco, "I can't go any farther."

Marco glanced down. They were a good ten, twelve feet off the ground. Sarah was about as high in the tree next to them, and Marco saw his mom and John in the tree on the other side of them. John shined his flashlight on the ground.

Marco realized he could no longer hear Ahab. The dog must have abandoned them. But what had made him yelp like that? He glanced down at the ground, where the flashlight beam illuminated, and nearly lost his grip on the tree.

Sarah screamed.

Below them were half a dozen brilliant orange crabs, the largest Marco had ever seen. Their legs were about three feet long, deadly looking claws snapping. One sidled its way to the pile of coconuts, selected one, then snapped it in two.

Marco's stomach churned.

"What are those things?" he asked.

John said, "I think they're giant coconut crabs."

For some reason, Marco felt relieved. As scary as they were, at least they were known creatures that had an actual name, unlike the red bird. Then he gulped. "Can they climb trees?"

John didn't answer the question. Instead, he said, "Find something you can use as a club."

Marco looked overhead and saw a solid branch about the size of his arm. He braced himself and managed to snap it off. He hefted it in his hand, then smacked the trunk of the tree.

*Crack!*

Not the best of weapons, but he could annoy one of those things if he had to, at least keep it from climbing up.

"Daddy?"

Sarah's voice wavered and Marco looked over at her. Her face was a pale oval, just visible in the branches. She was alone in the tree, and farthest from the fire. "What do I do?"

John called out, "Sweetie, you'll be fine. Can you find a branch?"

"Why?"

John was quiet for a moment, then finally said, "These things might want to climb one of our trees."

"What?" Sarah screeched. "Why?"

"It's okay," said Marco. "Find a stick like this one. See?" He held up the branch. "If they start to climb, you can just poke at them and they'll go back down." He had no idea if his theory was accurate, but it sounded pretty good.

Apparently, it was convincing enough for Sarah, who was whirling her head about, trying to find a weapon of her own. She reached up and grabbed a branch and pulled, but it resisted.

"Try again," urged Marco. "You can get it."

Sarah yanked again, but the thing didn't budge. Her shoulders slumped. "I can't!"

John's voice raised: "Marco!"

Marco swiveled around in his position and watched one of the crabs, what seemed like the biggest, head for the base of Sarah's tree. Marco realized his tree blocked Sarah's view, and that she wouldn't be able to see the crab until it was at the bottom of her trunk. He quickly said, “Let’s try another one.” He pointed behind her. “See that branch? Try that one.”

Sarah sighed and shifted until she saw the branch he was pointing to. She grabbed the branch and pulled. Marco saw it give a little, so he said, “That’s it!” He glanced down and saw the crab had reached Sarah’s tree.

The creature paused, one of its giant claws poised, snapping at the trunk.

Marco encouraged Sarah to try again. “Just one more good yank and you’ll have it.”

The crab put one leg up on the tree, then another, and began to climb up sideways.

Sarah pulled the branch free. With a bit of a smile on her face, she told Marco, “Got it.”

John called out, “I can’t see! What’s going on over there?”

Marco said, “Sarah, get a good grip on that thing.”

She froze. “Why?”

Marco pointed about four feet below her at the trunk, where the crab was making its way up.

Her eyes widened. “What do I do?”

“Wait till it gets close enough and then just . . .”

The crab was within three feet of Sarah when she reached down with her stick. The crab grabbed it with one pincer and Sarah pulled, heaving the crab off the trunk so that it was just hanging by the stick. Which it began to climb up.

Sarah screamed.

"Drop it!" Marco yelled. "Just drop it!"

Sarah let go and the crab plummeted to the ground, where it scurried back to the pile of coconuts. Then she wrapped her arms around herself.

"Sarah, you okay?" called her dad.

"No, I'm not okay!" she yelled. Her chin wobbled and her lips curled down. She began to cry.

Marco said, "That was scary."

She glared at him through her tears.

He added, "I don't know if I could have done what you did. That was brave."

She wiped her eyes and sniffled. "I didn't have time to think."

"Well, you did good," said Marco. He switched around so he could see his mom and stepfather. "What do we do now?"

John aimed the flashlight beam at the crabs, who seemed content with the pile of coconuts, snapping them open one after the other. He said, "I think we'd better get comfortable. Looks like we're going to spend the night in the trees."

# 19

The fire died out in the dim, wee hours of the morning, leaving Sarah in nearly complete blackness. The only light came from the moon that slipped slowly toward the horizon. Stiff from crouching in the branches for so long, she shifted her body, trying to find a more comfortable position. Her left leg had fallen asleep and began to tingle as it woke up. She patted and shook it until it felt normal, then she moved down a foot or so, to a wider branch, and lay down, her back to the massive trunk. The only good thing about the discomfort was that she'd finally stopped being terrified.

"You okay?" Marco was only a few feet away, but she couldn't see him.

She said, "As okay as you can be when you're stuck in a tree all night."

"Yeah, tell me about it."

Just then, there was a snore.

"Is that your brother?" asked Sarah.

Marco laughed a little. "Yeah. He can sleep through anything."

Sarah said, "I expected him to be more annoying. But he's pretty smart."

"Yeah, he is." He paused a moment. "But he can still be seriously annoying."

Sarah heard a rustle below her and sucked in a breath. "Are they back?"

There was a snuffle below, but she couldn't see what it was. Her imagination began to run, and her hands began to tremble as visions of Marco's weird bird and her kangaroo popped into her head. Along with those long-legged, scary crabs that looked like giant spiders—

A whine.

"Ahab?"

Marco said, "I see him!"

"Do you think it's safe to go down?" Sarah asked.

Her dad called from the other side of Marco's tree, "Is the dog back?"

"Yeah!" said Sarah. "Can we get down?"

Her dad didn't answer, but then a light shone up in Sarah's face. "I think we can get down. I'll build up the fire again." As Sarah started to edge down the tree, her dad held up an arm and helped her jump down. She stepped into him for a hug. "That was too scary."

Marco appeared beside them. "I'm gonna let him sleep." He pointed up.

John pointed the beam into the tree where Nacho had his head back against the tree trunk, snoring away. He laughed. "Let's get that fire going."

Yvonna called from her perch in the tree. "Is it okay to get down?"

Marco went over to her as Sarah put her arms around Ahab. "He knows, Dad."

"Knows what?" Her dad squatted by the fire pit, digging into the embers with a stick and trying to coax the fire back to life.

"He knows when there's danger." Sarah stood up and rubbed Ahab's giant head. "Don't you?" She took the flashlight and checked the dog all over for injuries, but found none. "You must have just gotten pinched, huh?"

Yvonna and Marco joined them, and sat down on some of the bedding that remained where they'd left it, still circling the fire. She said, "We should all try to get some sleep."

"Tonight was rough," said John. "If we're here for another night, I think that it would be wise to stay in that house Marco and I found."

Marco spoke up. "But I thought we needed to stay by the beach." His words were rushed. "I mean, we wouldn't want to miss a boat coming to rescue us."

The fire began to flame, and John added some wood to it, then sat down on the sand beside it. He looked at Marco. "It's just safer to be inside a structure."

Sarah said, "Yeah, way better than spending another night in a tree."

Yvonna said, "John, would you help me get Nacho down? He can't sleep the whole night up there." They left the fire to Marco, Sarah, and Ahab. Sarah looked over at Marco. "Why don't you want to stay in the house?"

Marco shrugged. "I just think we should stay here, in case a boat comes. Plus it's way too far to haul all our stuff."

Sarah glanced over at the pile of supplies. He had a point. "But we can't stay here." She shivered. "What if those crabs come back?"

Marco glanced over at the trees they'd just come

down from. "I think we could build a platform in those trees. We'd be off the beach that way, but still close enough in case a boat comes."

Sarah frowned. "How can we build something?"

Her dad came back carrying Nacho in his arms. He carefully laid the boy on the bedding and drew a blanket over him. "What are we building?"

Marco told him his idea and John began nodding. "I like it. We could salvage what wood we can from the boat, haul the berth mattresses and stuff up there . . ." He smiled. "Great idea."

Marco grinned and, to Sarah, he suddenly seemed far more at ease.

Nacho seemed to snore again immediately.

Yvonna said, "The rest of you need to get some sleep too."

John said, "I'll stay up and watch the fire, probably catch a nap sometime tomorrow."

Sarah snuggled down in her bed, being sure to keep one hand on Ahab, who had sprawled out next to her. As long as he was with them, she felt that at least she—that all of them—would have some kind of warning before whatever other danger lurking out there headed their way.

# 20

The sun was a glowing tangerine, low in the eastern sky, when Marco woke up. He was sweating under the blankets and threw them off, knowing the day was going to be a scorcher. Sarah and Nacho were still asleep, Ahab nestled between them, and his mom squatted by the fire, holding a small pan over it with one hand as she held a wooden spoon in the other, stirring.

Yvonna carried the pan back over to the makeshift kitchen, and busied herself putting something together. Marco went over to her and she handed him a bowl. "Breakfast?"

He peered inside. Sprinkled granola lay on top of a scoop of something pale and creamy with streaks of pink. "What is it?"

Yvonna smiled. "Well, I cooked up the guava into a sauce and strained it to get the seeds out, then put in some vanilla pudding snacks and topped it with granola. Just give it a try." She handed him a spoon.

He scooped up a small amount and tasted it. Crunchy, creamy, sweet, and just a tad tart. "I like it. Thanks."

She smiled. Then she put a hand over her mouth.

"Mom?"

"Oh. I think my stomach is still—" She turned and ran a little ways away, then dropped to her knees just out of sight behind a tree.

Marco wondered if she was throwing up again. He called out, "Mom? You okay?"

"Just a little queasy still," she called. "I'll be fine."

John came walking from down the beach. "Where's your mom?" he asked.

Marco wasn't sure his mom would want John to know she was sick, so he held up his bowl. "She made us breakfast and said she was going for a walk."

John picked up a bowl and took a spoonful. "This is tasty." He took a few more bites. "We're gonna need our strength."

Marco asked, "Are we going to the boat?"

John finished a mouthful. "I figured we could go into the hold from the hole in the side."

"That sounds dangerous," said Yvonna, who came walking up to them, looking much better than she had moments before.

"Mom," Marco said. "We're already shipwrecked on an island. I'm not sure how much more dangerous anything can get."

She smiled a little. "Point taken. But I'm still going to worry." She put her arm around his shoulders and squeezed. "I can't help it, so just deal with it."

"I'm pretty sure that thing is solid," John said. "But we'll be careful."

They finished eating. Marco helped John drag the dinghy down to the water and they rowed out to *Moonflight*. John said, "The water is so calm this morning. I should be able to get pretty close." He stowed the small oars and let the dinghy drift nearer to the ruined vessel.

Marco reached out with both arms and pushed against it. "Can you tie us off?"

John nodded, already reaching out with a rope. He looped it inside the hole in the hull, then pulled it tight. "I really don't think the boat is going anywhere. But I want you to stay out here, and if it moves at all, untie and row away, okay?"

Marco nodded.

John reached up and started pulling wood out, making the hole bigger. He tossed the remnants aside and groaned. "This is going to be harder than I thought. This is nowhere near big enough for me to get in."

"I can fit," said Marco.

John shook his head. "No way. Your mother would never speak to me again."

Marco didn't exactly see a problem with that, but he said, "She can't see us from here."

John didn't say anything, but Marco could tell from the expression on his face that he was considering it. So he added, "Really, I'll be fine. Plus I weigh less than you. I mean, if the boat was gonna move, it would be less likely to happen with me."

"Fine." John blew out a breath. "But you'd better be careful."

Marco nodded. "I will." He crawled over to the side of the dinghy nearest the hull and grabbed the side of the hole. He stuck one foot inside, making sure the footing was solid, then pulled himself the rest of the way inside. John handed him a flashlight.

Marco flitted the beam around the cabin. The space looked about the same as when they'd left it, only with about six inches of water everywhere; he slowly made his way to the captain's room. They had already collected the blanket off the bed, but he yanked on the thin mattress, which slid right off, and was easy enough to drag to the hole. But when he tried to fold it enough to fit through, the mattress filled the space, darkening the hold.

"Can you grab it?" he called to John. There was no answer, but the mattress left his hands and a few seconds later, the sun shined through again.

"Got it!"

Marco stuck his head out. The mattress nearly filled the dinghy. "Do you need to make a trip to shore?"

John shook his head. "I'm not leaving you out here."

"Lemme see what else I can find." Marco went back in. They had gotten most of the food supplies, but he found a canvas bag in the cupboard and filled it with whatever kitchen things they had left. In the next room, he noticed a book left on the shelf and stuffed it into the bag without looking at the cover. Then he went back into the captain's room. The trunk was there, and again he tried opening it. The lock didn't budge.

He curled his fingers around the leather handle on one end and yanked, expecting the trunk to be too heavy to move. But he was surprised at the lightness, and how easily he could move it in the water. He dragged the trunk to the hole, and then stepped into the sunlight. He handed the canvas bag to John. "Do you want more mattresses? There's no way they'll fit in the dinghy."

John rubbed his chin. "Yeah." He looked west, where clouds were building. "If we get another storm, this sailboat could sink. We better take all we can and then start pulling the wood."

Marco stepped back through the hole and dragged the trunk out.

John tilted his head as he looked at the trunk. "What is that?"

Suddenly, Marco felt embarrassed. Given their circumstances, it seemed insensitive—greedy almost—to be hauling out a possession of their captain's. "I think it was Captain Norm's." He shrugged.

His stepfather said, "Might as well bring it ashore. Maybe we can even get it back to Norm's family one day." He stepped forward and pulled on one handle as Marco pushed from behind. Once the trunk was settled, Marco scrambled aboard and helped John row back to shore. They unloaded and headed out to make another trip.

By the third trip, they'd retrieved everything of use from the vessel, so they headed back out to try and strip some wood. John lashed the dinghy's rope to the boat, then began yanking at the wood on the side of the hole. The storm had loosened everything, and after a battle with the first few, they were able to yank several more off and pile them in the dinghy.

John sat down and picked up the oars. "Let's take this load to shore. That's enough for today. We can rest up and come back for more tomorrow."

Marco asked, "We're giving up?"

John said, "No. But we had a long night and can't really build the platform today anyway."

If they couldn't get the rest of the wood, they couldn't build a platform in time for that night, so when those crabs came back . . .

Marco sighed and sat down.

John would make them go to that little house. Though the day was hot, Marco shivered.

# 21

As soon as her dad and Marco had started dumping loads on the beach, Sarah began sifting through them. More than willing to help with the day's task, she couldn't help but hope it took longer than expected, so that the platform wouldn't get built in the monkey pod trees and they'd be forced to go stay in the house that her dad and Marco had found.

She came upon the trunk. "Whoa." She ran a hand over a mermaid and smiled. "This is too cool." She jiggled the lock, to no avail. Maybe her dad would be able to get the thing open. For the time being, she gave up, sat down, and watched them row back to the beach. When they got close enough for her to see the dinghy didn't have nearly enough wood to build a platform, she stifled a grin and swallowed down the joy bubbling up in her throat. They would be in a building that night! Four walls, a roof, a floor . . . No vile, villainous crabs chasing them up into trees. She jogged down to the beach and met them. "Dad? Where's the rest of the wood?"

He patted her head. "I need to rest awhile." He glanced back out at the boat. "The platform will get built. Just not today."

Marco pointed at the sky. "What about the storm?"

John said, "Let's hope the boat is still standing after it hits."

Sarah's heart began to pound. "There's a storm coming?"

Nacho ran up to them. "Are we going to build a platform in the trees?"

"Not today," said John. "But maybe tomorrow."

"So we're sleeping on the beach again?" Nacho asked.

"No," blurted Sarah, and the three of them looked at her. "I mean, we can't right? If those crabs come back . . ."

Marco said, "We could build up the fire and be ready."

Sarah looked at her dad. She didn't want to sleep on the beach, and before she could stop it, her eyes filled with tears.

He set a hand on her head. "Last night was rough, huh?"

She nodded, unable to speak.

John looked at the boys, then back at her. "I think, just for tonight, we should pack it up and spend the night in the house we found."

Marco said, "But what if a ship comes and we're not here! It'll leave without us."

John shook his head. "That sky is looking darker all the time. A ship is not going to come through that, so I don't think we'll miss anything."

Marco didn't say anything as he walked away down the beach.

Sarah wiped her eyes and tried to smile. "What do we need to pack?"

At the pile of supplies, Sarah helped Yvonna stuff a few bags with food and water as her dad and the boys rolled up bedding into bundles they could carry. They stacked everything near the edge of the woods, then sat down for a meal of peanut butter and jelly on hot dog buns before heading out on their hike.

*BOOM!*

Ahab began barking.

Sarah glanced up and saw everyone looking at the sky behind her with wide eyes. Slowly, she turned. She dropped her bun in the sand and her legs nearly buckled beneath her.

The sky to the west was red.

Not like a sunset. Not even like a sunrise. Not like anything she'd ever seen. It was as if someone had squeezed a whole handful of cherries and let the juice drip down the entire western sky.

"Red sky at night, sailor's delight," recited Nacho. "Red sky at morning, sailors take warning." He shrugged. "There's no verse for middle of the day."

*Because there wasn't supposed to be a red sky at two in the afternoon.* Sarah's heart began to pound. "What is that?" she whispered.

Other than Ahab's constant barking, no one made a sound. Everyone simply watched.

Slowly the red streaks wrapped around each other, joining up, swirling together, moving faster and faster until they were a deep blur that suddenly stopped, a pulsing crimson orb in the sky. Then, it began moving straight for the beach.

John jumped up. "Grab what you can!" He shoved a backpack at Marco. "Run!"

Marco's jaw was slack, his eyes wide with fear. "Where?"

"To the house! Do you remember how to get there?"

Marco nodded. "Are you sure it will be safe enough?"

"There's nowhere else!" shouted John.

"The cave," said Marco.

Sarah shivered. She hated caves.

But her dad nodded and asked, "Do you know how to get there?"

"I remember."

John grabbed Nacho by the shoulder and shoved a canvas bag into his hands. "Take this and follow your brother." Nacho shifted the bundle and grabbed his backpack with his free hand, then ran after his brother to the trees.

Sarah threw on her backpack, grabbed a bundle of bedding, and began to run after them before her dad could even tell her to. Ahab ran beside her. As she reached the trees, she glanced back.

The smear of red had stalled, was simply a whirling mass hovering in the sky. Sarah breathed out in relief.

Ahab growled.

Suddenly, as if switching into gear, the orb surged, getting closer to the beach with every second. John and Yvonna scrambled, shoving things together.

Sarah yelled at them, "It's coming!"

They looked up, then took what they could carry and ran toward Sarah, who raced toward the trees.

Nacho's blue shirt was just visible ahead of her, and she aimed for that, trying to keep her footing in the tree roots and vines. Her heart pounded and she struggled to catch her breath. She'd lost it more from fear than exertion. What was that thing in the sky? And what would it do if—*when*—it reached the shore?

Sarah caught her foot on a vine and fell, landing on the bedding she carried. "*Ooommpphh!*" Ahab stuck his nose in her face.

Immediately, her dad was there, yanking her up by the arm. "Come on! Go! Go!"

Sarah grabbed her bundle. Nacho and Marco weren't in sight anymore. "Which way?"

Her dad paused. He was breathing hard and sweat ran down his face. He pointed. "That way. Follow right behind me."

With Ahab at her side, Sarah stayed on her dad's heels and she heard Yvonna running behind her. Just when Sarah didn't think she could run any further, they emerged in a clearing. He stopped abruptly.

Sarah looked past him to Marco and Nacho. Beside them, the dark mouth of a cave yawned, and her dad pointed the flashlight inside.

"Hurry!" Marco yelled.

Sarah reeled around.

The red orb was above the treetops, getting nearer and growing bigger. She ran into her dad's back as she tried to squeeze into the cave behind him, everyone else crowding in after them, their panting loud in the enclosed space. The flashlight didn't light more than a few feet in front of them, but her dad kept going, away from the mouth of the cave, Ahab at his side. There seemed to be nothing but steep walls on either side of them, and after about fifty yards, the walls widened into a room. Her dad stopped and turned to face them. "Let's stop here."

Sarah glanced behind them. "Are we far enough in?"

As if to answer her, Ahab moved to the edge of their light, looking back the way they'd come. He tilted his head and froze. No one said anything, and Sarah realized she was holding her breath.

Then Ahab's tail began to wag slightly and he turned around to face them. He sat down on his haunches and panted. Sarah breathed out. "I think it's safe." She dropped her load of bedding and collapsed on top of it, hoping that she was right.

# 22

Marco breathed in, but the air seemed to stick halfway down, not letting him get as much as he wanted. With shaking hands, he picked up a bottle of water and drank, trying to calm himself. *Don't think about it*, he told himself. But he couldn't help it.

Ever since they'd arrived at the island, what was supposed to be their safe haven, one strange thing after another had happened. First, there had been the red bird. And then the glass bottle and the woman's voice. Then, just before dinner, that weird wail. And of course the Attack of the Monster Crabs, followed by the sleepless night, and then . . .

That red thing in the sky.

Goose bumps sprouted on his arms. He took another swig of water. *Think about something else.*

His mom was spreading out the few blankets and pillows they'd carried with them, while Sarah helped John make some sandwiches.

Marco's stomach churned. He couldn't even think about eating.

His gaze went to Ahab, who was asleep. He couldn't help but think that if something bad was going to happen, the dog wouldn't be so calm, right? Marco glanced at the entrance to their part of the cave, which was in shadow.

He was glad they chose the cave instead of the house. Something about that place gave him the creeps. Not that the cave was that homey, but it just seemed like it had less of . . . a history. When he was around the house, he couldn't shake the feeling that whoever had lived there before wouldn't want them there.

"Marco?" Nacho sat down by him. "How long do you think we'll have to stay in here?"

Marco shrugged. "No clue."

His little brother whispered, "Someone is gonna have to go look out there, right?" His eyebrows knotted and he sucked in part of his lip.

Marco gently elbowed him. "Not for a while. It was probably just some weird weather."

"Seriously?" Nacho didn't look convinced.

"Sure." Marco nodded. "We're totally safe in here."

His mom asked John, "What was that thing?"

Marco's stepfather scratched his head. "Maybe some weird weather thing?"

Marco raised his eyebrows at Nacho, as if to say *See? I told you.* But Marco didn't believe for a second that any weather had caused that red thing. He'd seen; it had *chased* them.

He looked over at Sarah. She had a skeptical look on her face that showed she didn't think it was the weather either. She spoke up. "Something is going on with this place." She looked pointedly at Marco. "Tell them."

Marco's mouth dropped open, and he quickly snapped it shut. He frowned. "Tell them what?"

Her eyes narrowed. "What you saw. In that house."

Both Yvonna and John peered at him, waiting. He wasn't about to tell them about the bird or the perfume. And he definitely wasn't going to tell them about the woman's voice. What good would it do? Even if he wasn't going crazy, and he really *had* seen and heard those things, telling the others would only make things worse. He had no idea how long they would be on that island, and scaring everyone even more would not help things at all.

Sarah said, "Come on! Don't you think after what you told me, and then that red thing in the sky—" She pointed toward the cave entrance. "Don't you think you should tell them?"

"Marco?" asked his mom. "What did you see?"

"Nothing." He shook his head and gestured toward John. "He was there. We didn't see anything."

"The bird!" said Sarah. "Tell them about that."

Her dad asked, "The bird in the fireplace?"

Sarah's forehead wrinkled. "You saw it?"

Her dad shook his head. "Not exactly." He asked Marco, "What about the bird?"

Marco shrugged and tried to sound matter-of-fact and calm, about the opposite of what he was actually feeling. "I have no idea what she's talking about. It was just a bird."

"No it wasn't!" cried Sarah. "He told me."

Marco felt bad as he forced a smile. "It was a joke. I was trying to freak you out." He shrugged. "Sorry if you thought I was serious."

"You were!" Sarah glared at him. "I could tell."

"How? You've known me for like three days!" He held up his palms. "I was just messing around."

Tears welled up in Sarah's eyes, and she crossed her arms and plopped down, facing away from all of them. Her dad went and sat beside her, and put an arm around her shoulders.

Marco swallowed. Sarah was right. And although he felt bad for being mean, he just wasn't ready to let the others know the truth . . . that something was seriously off about the island.

And that he believed they were in far more danger than anyone suspected. But they were already alert to some dangers, and had already found a safe place to stay. So what difference would it make whether or not he told them everything? His mom was already scared enough; he didn't want to make it any worse for her. Or his little brother.

# 23

Sarah sat down on the bedding and fumed. She didn't believe for a second that Marco had lied to her about what he'd seen. But if he'd told her the truth, that meant he was lying to their parents. And Nacho. But why?

"Are you mad at him?"

"Huh?" Sarah asked.

Nacho dropped a beach towel beside her and plopped down on top of it. "My brother. He can be a pain sometimes."

Sarah huffed. "Sometimes?"

Nacho nodded. "Yeah." He pulled off his backpack and set it in his lap. He unzipped it and pulled out a bottle of hand sanitizer. He used some, then held up the bottle to Sarah. She stuck out her hand.

Sarah rubbed her hands together as she watched him pull out a notebook. "What's that?"

"My Eco-Scout stuff. I'm trying to earn badges, so I have to study a lot." He flipped open the notebook.

"You did a great job starting the fire." Sarah was sincere, because she'd been very impressed. She knew she wouldn't have been able to do it.

"Thanks," said Nacho. "It's kind of the first outdoor thing I've done."

Sarah frowned. "But I thought Eco-Scouts were all about the outdoors."

"Yeah, they are. I'm not that comfortable in the outdoors, I guess." He shrugged.

She smiled at him. "Well, you could have fooled me."

"Really?" He raised his eyebrows.

She nodded.

He smiled, then began to page through the notebook.

Sarah asked, "Is that more boating stuff?"

"No." He shook his head. "I'm kinda trying to get my mind off that for the moment."

Sarah nodded. "I get that. So what is it?"

Nacho pointed at a page. "I'm studying for my astronomy badge."

Sarah frowned. "I thought Eco-Scouts were just about the Earth. I mean, our planet." She shrugged. "It is the only one we have, right?"

"Maybe not." Nacho's eyes widened and he lowered his voice to almost a whisper. "Scientists think that the first truly Earth-like alien planet is going to be spotted next year."

"What?" Sarah scrunched up her nose. "We're on the only Earth."

Nacho shook his head. "That's what we've thought all this time."

"But what would happen if they found another . . . Earth?"

Nacho swallowed and said, even more quietly, "We would have to rethink our place in the universe."

Sarah wondered what that would be like, to know there was another Earth out there, maybe even with a girl like her living a parallel life. Was that even possible? She rolled her eyes. "Are you just messing with me?"

"No!" Nacho shook his head. "Really, I'm not. Check this out." He flipped through his notebook and pulled out a newspaper clipping. "See? Back in 1995 they found the first planet that had a sun like ours. And since then, they've found more than eight hundred worlds beyond our solar system. In the last few years, astronomers have found several exoplanets that have one or two of the same traits as Earth."

She asked, "What's an exoplanet?"

Nacho said, "Planets outside our solar system."

"Oh." Sarah looked at the clipping, a black-and-white photo of a tiny planet. "Like what kind of traits?"

Nacho shrugged. "Like size or surface temperature." He paged through and pulled out another clipping. "Here."

Sarah skimmed the article, which was an interview with an astronomer. She stopped and went back to re-read one part: the part where he said he was certain Earth's twin would be discovered in the next year. She looked up at Nacho. "Is this for real?"

Nacho nodded. "Since the Kepler Space Telescope launched, it's flagged more than twenty-three hundred potential planets."

"What's a potential planet?" asked Sarah.

"It might just end up being an asteroid or something," explained Nacho. "So they have to follow up, make sure it's the real deal."

She handed the clipping back to him. "So what happens if they find one? It's not like we have a spaceship to get there."

Nacho shrugged. "Maybe we won't have to."

"Why?" asked Sarah.

"Because whoever lives on those planets might be smarter than we are. They might already know how to come to us." Nacho buried his head back in the notebook.

Weird kid, thought Sarah. But then maybe she wasn't giving him enough credit. He knew a lot of stuff she hadn't known when she was ten. She smiled. Actually, he knew a lot of stuff she didn't know *now*. She was rather glad he was there, although she wished his older brother wasn't.

And she reached into her own backpack and pulled out Harry Potter, hoping that some time at Hogwarts would help take her mind off the fact that they were stuck in a cave on a deserted island that was turning out to be stranger and stranger the longer they stayed.

# 24

Marco shivered and pulled on his sweatshirt. With him wearing only a T-shirt and board shorts—and after sweating in the heat of the day—the chill air inside the enclosed space was not easy to get used to. But despite the dank and clammy cave, and the faint sound of constantly dripping water, Marco found himself content for the moment. They were safe and dry and whatever was outside didn't seem to be coming for them.

John had charged two solar flashlights from the boat earlier that day, and they shone brightly, lighting up the cave to the level of a bunch of candles. Ahab was asleep, leading Marco to believe they weren't in any danger at the moment.

His mom came over to him and held out a granola bar. "Hungry?"

Actually, he was famished. "Thanks." Marco unwrapped it and took a bite. He asked, "How long are we gonna stay in here?"

His mom shrugged. "I don't know."

John was only a few feet away and said, "I was thinking of checking in a little while."

Yvonna frowned. "You can't go out there! What if—"

"What?" asked Marco.

"I don't know," she said. "What if that thing, whatever it was, is right outside the cave? What do we do then?"

Marco ate the rest of his snack, crumpled up the wrapper, and set it down beside him. He got to his feet and told his stepfather, "Let's go check."

"No," said his mom.

Sarah and Nacho were a few feet away, reading, and they both looked up. Sarah asked, "We're leaving?"

"No, we're not," said Yvonna.

John set a hand on her arm. "We do have to check eventually. We can't stay in here forever." He glanced at his watch. "Almost five. We've been in here a few hours."

Marco said, "I think we should check."

John stood up. "So do I." He smiled down at his wife before she could protest. "Marco and I will go and we'll be careful."

As if he'd been invited, Ahab stood up, stretched, and lined up in front of them, ready to lead the way.

"See? We'll be fine." Before his mom could stop him, Marco picked up one of the flashlights and headed for the passageway to the cave entrance.

His stepfather called out, "Hey, wait up."

Marco paused so he could catch up, and handed him the flashlight. "You better go first or my mom will have a fit."

"I heard that," said his mom.

He smiled at her. "Mom, we'll be fine."

She just shook her head and sank down beside Nacho and Sarah.

Marco followed John up the passageway, which seemed longer now that they weren't hurrying like before. In fact, Marco wondered whether they could go any slower, but then he realized Ahab was being cautious on purpose. He asked John, "Do you think it's safe?"

He didn't answer at first. Then he said, "I hope it is. I mean, it's a little hard to tell. It's not exactly like a thunderstorm passing, is it?"

Marco didn't have a reply, so he followed the dog and John and the glow of the flashlight in silence. As they neared the entrance, their path grew lighter, and then they were mere steps from outside. Ahab ran outside.

John handed Marco the flashlight. "Take this. If anything happens, you run back to your mom and the others, okay?"

Marco nodded, his fingers folding tightly around the flashlight. He stayed right behind John as he took the final steps to the entrance and leaned out.

Marco held his breath.

John popped back in so fast that Marco jumped. "What? What did you see?"

His stepfather smiled. "Nothing. Looks like it looked before."

Marco stepped around him and walked outside. Ahab stood in the clearing, his nose in the air, sniffing. His tail wagged. Above the trees the sky was blue and free of clouds and, more important, *normal.* He grinned. That red orb was nowhere to be seen.

John said, "Stay right here with Ahab, I'll go get the others." He took the flashlight and disappeared back into the cave.

Marco took a few more steps into the clearing and

patted Ahab on the head. The trees, and maybe the island itself, no longer seemed sinister. Well, for the moment anyway, until another danger showed up. How funny, he thought, that everything about the island seemed *better* almost, now that one scary, unknown thing had been eliminated.

Ahab barked, but didn't show any inclination to run off. He barked again.

"What's wrong?" Marco didn't see anything in the trees.

A few minutes later, everyone piled out of the cave.

Yvonna asked, "Where are we going?"

John said, "I still think the house is a good idea for the rest of the day."

"Beats that cave," said Sarah.

Before Marco could say anything, they heard a scream. Not like the sound the day before. This one was more human. More like a real scream.

And it came from the direction of the beach.

# 25

The sound of the scream made Sarah's heart pound. "Where is that coming from?"

"Sounds like the beach," said her dad. "Everyone, grab your stuff." He began to head that way.

"Wait!" she yelled. "Why are we going toward it?" The vision of that blood-colored ball in the sky still haunted her.

Her dad said, "Someone could be hurt. Maybe a boat came during the . . . storm."

*Storm?* thought Sarah. *That thing was no storm and everyone knew it.* But they all followed her dad as he headed back toward the beach. She took a look around, realized she was not about to stay there by herself, and had to jog to catch up.

After a moment, they no longer heard the scream. Sarah called ahead to the others, "It stopped! I don't think we should go any farther."

Her dad was in front, just behind Ahab, and he stopped and turned around. He was breathing a little hard from the heat and the exertion, and he took a moment to wipe sweat off his red face. "We really need to check it out, sweetie. You could stay here."

"No way." Sarah shook her head. As the others began moving again, she followed, just wanting to get it over with.

They emerged on the beach a few moments later, and Ahab tore off down the sand, rounding the first corner where he disappeared. John and Marco dropped their things and jogged after him, while Nacho and Yvonna carried their things to their abandoned camp. She said, "I think we should stay here."

Nacho nodded. "I'll take care of the fire."

Sarah set her things down and said, "I'm gonna follow them."

Yvonna said, "Maybe you should stay here."

All the more reason to go, thought Sarah. "I want to be with my dad." She jogged down the beach and around the corner. Her dad and Marco were just down the beach, crouched in the sand as Ahab barked beside them. Sarah sped up until she nearly reached them. She stopped and leaned over to catch her breath, then started to ask, "What—"

Then she saw what lay between them on the sand.

A girl.

Her dark skin glistened with sweat, and her thick, ebony hair was in two massive braids that reached nearly to her waist. Under an orange T-shirt her chest heaved, but her eyes remained closed. The girl wore bright pink-and-orange-flowered shorts, and her feet were bare, the soles caked with sand.

"Dad?" asked Sarah. "Who is that?"

Her dad shook his head but didn't look at her. He set a hand on the girl's forehead. "She's so hot."

Marco asked, "Do you think she's the one who screamed?"

John looked down the beach. "Yeah."

"Where did she come from?" asked Sarah. Then she noticed footprints that had to belong to the girl. They had come from down the beach, around the next corner, where Sarah thought she had seen the kangaroo. She took a few steps that way and looked down.

"Look! She left a message in the sand!"

Scrawled into the sand at her feet were the words:

BEWARE THE C

A stick lay next to the *C*, as if the girl dropped it before she could finish the message.

Marco stood next to Sarah. "It's a warning."

"She didn't get a chance to finish it." She asked Marco, "What do you think she was trying to say? Beware the *C*. What starts with *C*?" Then her eyes widened. "Crabs! Coconut crabs! Maybe she was warning us about them."

"Maybe," said Marco. He didn't seem convinced. "She must have seen our camp or the fire and realized there were people here. And she wanted to leave us a message."

They all gazed at the girl, who was still unconscious.

Just then, the wail arose, that same grief-stricken keening of the day before. Sarah covered her ears, as did her dad and Marco.

"It's the same time as yesterday!" Marco yelled.

Sarah felt the sound in her chest, biting through

her. She shut her eyes, trying to close out the sound. "What is that?!" Sarah looked at her dad and Marco, and they all stood there, hands over their ears, until the sound stopped.

They dropped their hands.

John put one arm around the girl's back, the other under her legs, and lifted her up. Her head sagged into his chest, and he told Marco and Sarah, "Come on. Let's get back to the fire." He headed toward their camp.

But Marco and Sarah stayed there, looking at the words in the sand, a panting Ahab between them.

Marco asked, "What is with this place?"

Sarah looked sideways at him. "You lied earlier."

He nodded.

"To me or them?" She swallowed. "Did you really see the bird?"

"Yeah, I did," he said.

Sarah crossed her arms. "Then why did you say that you didn't?"

He held out his palms. "Mom and Nacho are so freaked out. And my mom hasn't been feeling well. I didn't want to worry them anymore. Everything was kind of weird already, and—"

"And you think after that thing in the sky . . ." She

looked up the beach, at her dad carrying the girl. "And her." She pointed at the words. "And that? You think they won't get suspicious?" She shook her head. "This isn't Disneyland."

"There's something I didn't tell you. Something I haven't told anyone." Marco reached into the pouch of his sweatshirt and held up the bottle.

Sarah squinted. "What is that?"

"I think that it's some kind of perfume."

Sarah started to open it.

Marco tried to grab it back. "Don't—!"

But she already had the stopper off, and held up the bottle to take a whiff. Her lips began to curve, but then the smile froze halfway. Sarah's eyes widened and she stared at Marco.

He whispered, "You heard it? The voice?"

Slowly, Sarah nodded. "She said, *Come back*." She replaced the lid and couldn't hand the bottle back to Marco fast enough. "Where did you get that?"

"The house." Marco put the bottle back in his pocket.

"Is that why you didn't want to go back there?" asked Sarah.

He nodded. "Something is wrong with this place. This island."

"I know," said Sarah. "Did you notice . . ."

"What?"

Sarah motioned up at the sky. "Birds."

Marco looked up. "I don't see any."

She nodded. "Exactly. When we were on the boat, they were all over. But here . . ."

Marco breathed out slowly. "When we found the waterfall and the pool, it was so beautiful. So *perfect*. But something just felt off. And that's what it is. This place is too quiet."

"Way too quiet," said Sarah. "There's nothing here, other than those crabs and your bird and my kangaroo—"

"Your *what*?" Marco frowned.

Sarah described what she'd seen. "But I could have imagined it." Even as she said it, even as she *hoped* it, she knew it wasn't true. "This freaks me out, but . . . I believe it was real."

"So do I." Marco gazed out at the water. "But you know what really scares me?"

Sarah wasn't sure she wanted to know. But she asked anyway. "What?"

His eyes locked with hers. "I have a feeling that we haven't seen the worst of this place. Not at all." He began walking back to camp.

A breeze picked up, puffing at Sarah's face and flicking her hair up off her shoulders. Ahab growled, and a chill ran up Sarah's spine. "It's okay, boy. It's okay." Then, knowing that she was dead wrong, that nothing at all about that island was even in the same ballpark as *okay,* she jogged after Marco, Ahab at her heels.

Thank you for reading this Feiwel and Friends book.

The Friends who made

# SHIPWRECK ISLAND

possible are:

JEAN FEIWEL, Publisher

LIZ SZABLA, Editor in Chief

RICH DEAS, Senior Creative Director

HOLLY WEST, Associate Editor

DAVE BARRETT, Executive Managing Editor

NICOLE LIEBOWITZ MOULAISON, Production Manager

LAUREN A. BURNIAC, Editor

ANNA ROBERTO, Associate Editor

CHRISTINE BARCELLONA, Administrative Assistant

Follow us on Facebook or visit us online at mackids.com.

OUR BOOKS ARE FRIENDS FOR LIFE.